Glasgow Underground & Nicotine
by Andy Reilly

All Rights Reserved. No part of this publication may be reproduced in any form or by any means, including scanning, photocopying, or otherwise without prior written permission of the copyright holder. Copyright ©️ 2013

The Glasgow Underground & Nicotine is a collection of short stories and mutterings based on the everyday lives in the city.

You'll laugh, you'll cry, you'll sometimes wonder what the hell it's all about. And then when you've put up with everything that Glasgow has to offer, you can read this book and realise that there are plenty of folk that are worse off than yourself.

It's a Glasgow book with the proverbial chip on its shoulder...but at least the chip isn't covered in salt n sauce.

As with so many things in life, you get an idea and it nags away at you for quite a while. Eventually you get started and then a long time after that, you eventually get the first draft finished.

And then two days later one of the key reasons you started pulling the collection together passes away. This isn't a book about the Velvets and there is no great connection other than a love of the band and a love of puns. If you're looking for a book about Lou, the band or their debut album, this isn't it.

However, I hope you have a read through, it's a lighthearted book combining the light and the dark, the good and the bad.

And with that in mind...This one's for you Lou.

THE GLASGOW UNDERGROUND & NICOTINE

"Gonna take a walk down to George Square, you never know who you're gonna find there"

Eleven short stories based in Glasgow from the great and the good to the sick and dirty, sometimes more dead than alive. It's time to revisit the people from all the streets you crossed, not so long ago.

Sunday Mourning
I'm Hating On That Bam
Farmfood's Al
Venus In Firhill
Run Ron Run
All Jo Morrow's Panties
Heroes Inn
George Square She Goes Again
She'll Be Your Mirror
The Blane Valley Death Song
You're No Peeing Son

Andy Reilly

Contents

Sunday Mourning..5
I'm Hating On That Bam..17
Farmfood's Al 26
Venus In Firhill..37
Run Ron Run..55
All Jo Morrow's Panties..65
Heroes Inn..77
George Square She Goes Again..88
She'll Be Your Mirror 97
The Blane Valley Death Song...103
You're No Peeing Son...108

Sunday Mourning

As a Glaswegian man, hitting 26 could legitimately qualify you for a midlife crisis so finally stumbling upon it at 38 wasn't the most careless outcome in the grand scheme of things; it was almost as if you cheated the system for over a decade. However, when it hits, it hits hard, and it often hits in the strangest of fashions.

When it kicks in, it often manifests itself in the same old ways. Trading your car in for a younger model, trading your wardrobe in for a fresher look or even ditching your good lady for a far younger, perkier and far less intelligent model. It's a cliché but acting out in this fashion, as tragic as it seems, is somewhat acceptable. Terry Shields though, he had no intention of going through the regular motions.

It helps a bit when you don't drive, and you're already on wife number 2 because the first one was a crabbit arse, but when other men were trying to turn back the hands of time, Terry laid down and let himself be beaten over the head with the mallet of passing time. For two whole days, he stayed in bed...another reminder of moving on because it used to be that spending two whole days in bed was a sign of a great weekend but now, it was all down to the fact that the weekends never happened round here anymore.

It was a normal Monday like any other in the office, or so it seemed. The Evening Times was running through its usual nonsense, moaning about the traffic in Glasgow, showcasing what D-list Glaswegian celebrity was turning up for the opening of a crisp-poke and shining a light onto the leading stars of a local community network that deserved to be hidden away for its own good. In between all the guff but before the Garfield cartoon strip, a story caught Terry's eye.

CLUBBERS OPT-IN FOR LAST TIME

"The queues were around the block last night as popular Glasgow DJs call it quits with The Sub Club saying goodbye to Optimo."

Terry didn't bother reading the rest, the picture of the queue snaking its way past the Crystal Palace and the headline was enough. The annoyance of missing the club's last night was unfortunate enough, but the fact that he never knew about it was a bigger shock. Even though it had been a few years since Terry had popped along, he had always meant to head back, he had always thought he had stayed in touch with the club and its culture. Now clearly this wasn't the case, Terry like so many others, had found life got in the way of clubbing, but it seems as though the one true club he had a love for had finished before there was a chance to dance one more night, hear one more tune, one more tune, one more tune.

A small and dark room used to provide the highlight of Terry's week, but that night, when he got home from work on autopilot, he put himself to bed and never got out until late on Wednesday evening. Even then, that was purely because he was manhandled out of there.

"Look Terry, you can't stay in bed all week," said his long-suffering wife, Annie.

"I've got plenty of holiday days left, god knows we're not going to bloody use them, I could have…" Terry paused, as though the effort of finishing the sentence was too much for him. He looked around, his eyes slowly becoming accustomed to the light streaming in from the hall, "I could have…that'll be on my bloody gravestone."

"Now come on Terry, we'll have less of that sort of talk, you know fine well we're getting you cremated when you pop off" chuckled Annie but Terry was unmoved by the thought.

He wasn't in the mood for moving at all. Annie explained that he had better get himself washed and looking half respectable as his pal James was making his way over. Terry had barely hauled himself into the shower before he heard the front door go. "That bugger can wait as well," said Terry under his breath as he cleaned himself for the first time since Monday morning.

Before too long, Terry was planting himself down on the settee in the living room as James finished off his first tea of his visit. No matter the visit, James ran through a lot of drinks if it was a school night, there was a lot of tea to be consumed. If there was no work to look forward to in the morning, it was the more traditional T that was being knocked back.

"So I hear you've been a bit down mate?" opened James, obviously deciding that this was not a time for pussyfooting about the subject matter. Annie had had a word with him over the phone, and two things had shocked him about the story. First of all, it really wasn't like Terry to miss his work and stay in his bed. Secondly, and much more shockingly, it certainly wasn't like Terry to have a shower just for James coming over. He clearly had been hiding away for a few days if he needed to clean up to that extent.

Terry eventually got around to responding to his mate, "Did you know it was finishing on Sunday?"
James looked at his friend blankly, oblivious to what Terry was on about. "What finished on Sunday?"

"Optimo."

The one word answer brought a smile to James' face. "Optimo. What a club that was we had some brilliant nights in there. Still, when was the last time we were there, it must have been back in 2006?"

Terry then unloaded. He always clung to the fact that it was still going and that he still felt in touch with the kids and what was happening. With Optimo gone, there wasn't a club night in Glasgow that Terry was interested in attending. His clubbing days were over, and that scared the life out of him.

With that, Terry stood up and announced he was going back to his bed.

James just sat there stunned, finished the last of his tea and placed it on the table in front of him. All of this over a club, sure it was a brilliant laugh at the time, but it was not as if we were there every week or were regular faces that everyone knew. It was just a decent night that we went to when we could.

Annie came in and noticing that Terry was nowhere to be seen turned her attention to James. James scratched his head, looked at Annie and said, "As daft as it sounds hen, he's upset by a club night closing down."

Annie took a seat, "I've never even been to a club with him, I didn't know he liked that." James ran through their old clubbing days while Annie explained that she was more of a Bonkers type of girl. James thought about joking that Terry always seemed to end up with bonkers lassies, but he never quite knew how to take Annie. She had been beneficial for Terry, there was no doubting that, a claiming influence at a time when he needed that the most but it took him away from his old lifestyle into the next. That's not a bad thing, only certain folk can head to clubs all their days without looking as though they are for the watching and James and Terry were not part of that modest clientele.

"He'll be fine hen, it's just reminded him that he's getting old. Mine happened when my dad died, so everyone was supportive anyway, it just seems strange cos it's a daft thing, but it comes to us all" was all that James could offer before he headed off. That seemed like a reasonable explanation but when did reasonable explanations ever have part in a marriage?

As she sat herself down with a cup of tea and some idiotic soap on the telly, Annie started questioning herself and all of the stories that her pals had told her before she got hitched to Terry. "Don't marry a divorced guy Annie, it'll have been his fault, and if he strays once, he'll stray again." "He's not to be trusted Annie, look at him and his pals, a bunch of wrong uns."

And so on and so forth. She'd had her arguments with Terry, of course she did, Annie would have been more worried if she never had arguments with people but to take himself off to bed on his own for a couple of days, no that's not right. Terry had taken the next few days off work on annual leave, the annual leave he was bemoaning at not using for Monday, so he wouldn't be in trouble with his work. That's fine, but it was a bloody waste thought Annie. Even if the two of them never got away, they could have had a couple of days off at the same time, heading into town for some lunch, being a bit more relaxed as they cut about the shops together. She knew he seemed down, but when your thoughts are on your man being a bloody waster and a selfish one at that, it was hard for Annie to show Terry any sympathy.

So with that, as the time came for her to go to bed, she decided that she would be better off on the couch. She hauled the spare blanket and pillows from out of the cupboard and settled down for an uncomfortable night on the couch. At some point in the middle of the night, Terry awoke, looked at the alarm clock and realised that Annie wasn't beside him. He initially thought that she must have been to the toilet, but when he stretched out; her side of the bed was as cold as a bottle of Corona that had been forgotten about in the back of the fridge. "Brilliant" thought Terry, "I'm right in the dog house now" but he was soon snoring once again.

If Terry thought that Annie's side of the bed was cold during the middle of the night, it was nothing like the frosty reception that awaited him as he made his way into the kitchen in the morning. Given the fact that he was up and out of his bed, this should have been seen as progress, but it seemed like a massive step backwards.

"Any tea or toast for me hen?" asked Terry but Annie snapped back, "Naw, get yer ain."

"Haw darling, I'm sorry…that news really took it out of me on Monday, I'm getting older hen."

"A bloody club night that you hadn't been to in at least 5 years. You don't even listen to that sort of music in the house. We watch X Factor on a Saturday night and suddenly you're telling me that you're some sort of secret raver who misses the days of going dancing…what is it really Terry, is it me?"

This struck Terry hard. "Naw hen, of course not" in fact, it was only at this point that Terry had realised how much that it was not about Annie. He had barely given her a thought since he read that Optimo had ended. She wasn't part of that life; she hadn't met that Terry, so it was nothing to do with her. Best not to explain it in that manner thought Terry though, "Look hen, that was a large part of my life, and that's it done now though. It doesn't mean that I don't like my life now, it's so much better, it was just a wee bit of a shock. It would have been good to have gone along, said one big goodbye to that sort of nonsense and fun."

It was an honest answer, not always the best policy, but it seemed to have struck a chord with Annie.

"Look Terry, I'll stand by you through most things, but you've got to be honest with me. We've not got kids so if you're missing other women or wanting to give that another chance, it'll take not long for me to get you kicked out of this house and off the title deeds."

"Annie....look hen, we were made for each other, we probably even deserve each other. This isnae about you, it's about the old days and thinking about what I used to get up to. I used to get pished on cheap cider down the park when I was 14. I kinda miss having no responsibility, but I don't want to go back there. I miss seeing the look of daft Shuggie's face the first time he tried hair lacquer and milk, but I never want to try that concoction again. All they daft things I said goodbye to when I acted like an adult and started going clubbing. This is now the stage where I'm saying goodbye to acting like a daft adult and starting to settle down a bit. It's just.... I just never really got to say the goodbye bit. I'm sorry hen."

"You get back to your bed Terry, I'll bring you up some tea and toast in a few minutes." Terry gave his missus a hug and a kiss and then grabbed the paper which she hadn't finished reading. "Oi you...cheeky" chided Annie, but she was starting to make a plan. Later that day, she made a phone call to James and the two of them hatched a plan for Friday evening.

By Thursday afternoon, Terry was feeling a bit better about life and decided that he needed to do something to make it up to Annie. "Look love, why don't we go out for a meal on Friday night, maybe go to the pictures?"

"Oh Terry, that sounds lovely, but I've made plans to go to my sisters. When you were lying low at the start of the week, I didn't know how long you'd be out of the game for so I made other plans, no point in me wasting my Friday night...next week eh?"

Terry was a bit disappointed, Annie was never one to turn down the offer a dinner and a movie. "I'll just put the kettle on love," said Annie as she moved into the kitchen and text James. Within a minute, Terry's mobile phone rang.

"Awright tadger, you oot yer bed yet?" said the voice through the phone and Terry laughed. The two of them were cracking on about the old times and seeing as Annie was busy on Friday night, Terry decided to go out for a few pints with James, well, if Annie would let him.

"Aye, the two of you get yourself out for an evening. Actually, I cannae be bothered making your dinner, why don't the two of you get some pub grub….somewhere cheap though, you'll need your money to take me out the following week." And with that, it was all falling into place. The boys were going into town for a few drinks, some scran and Annie was heading over to her sisters for an evening there, or at least so Terry thought. "Cool, tell you what mate, seeing as we're on an old school kick, lets grab some food in the Crystal Palace and then we'll head into McSorleys, get some pre-club drinks" suggested James and this may be the sort of nostalgia that Terry was looking for.
Friday came around and Annie had been out for most of the day getting some stuff for her sister.
They bloody sisters thought Terry, never aff the phone, never going two or three days without seeing each other and yet it was like a military operation anytime they were meeting up. Terry was in the middle of getting himself ready for heading out when Annie breezed in through the front door. Popping down to see her, he sees a 24 pour pack of Tennents sitting on the kitchen table.

"What's this?" asked Terry and Annie replied "Well, after you two get some scran and a few pints, why don't you just head back here for some more drinks. It'll be cheaper, you'll avoid the dafties oot on a Friday night, you can have a conversation, you can choose the music, and you don't have

12

to wait for a taxi or be stuck with idiots on the late bus. Also, it'll keep you away from any daft lassies" laughed Annie.

What a woman thought Terry, she's a keeper…and not just because of her gigantic hands and her ability to punch things away from danger, she actually was worth holding on to. "Cheers hen, I promise we'll have a big night next week, I love you, you know." Terry turned away to continue getting ready, and Annie was close to tears at the big idiot, aye, she loved him as well. Of course she did given all the things that she was doing for him.

Before too long, Terry was all set and good to go. "Right love, you have a good night," said Annie before kissing him goodbye and practically kicking him out of the door. As Terry made his way to the bus stop, Annie made her way to the computer and the emails that she had received from James.
In town, the buzz of an early Friday had well and truly kicked in. Let's face it, with Glasgow City Council workers clocking off around 11.30am on a Friday, there were plenty of folk who had been getting into the weekend vibe for quite a while. Terry and James just about managed to find a table and before two long, two burgers and a couple of pints were making their way to table 84.

"Here, it is cracking value in here, I'll need to bring Annie in some time," said Terry. James responded immediately, "She'll no thank you for it mate, value is not a watchword that comes with romance. We think a burger and a pint for less than a fiver, cracking, she sees it as a cheap date and a sign that you're saving money for another lassie. Honestly mate, it's not worth the hassle, take her somewhere you get a lot less food for more money."

Aaah, the confusing perplexities of womenfolk, no matter what age Terry lives to, he'll never understand it. The Crystal Palace was heaving with all sort of Glaswegian life. The old jakies who are in every day were still kicking about, coaxing the last of their last pint before heading off into the chilly evening breeze. The office workers were in letting their hair down after a rough week, no doubt someone was setting themselves up for an awkward week ahead by being drunk, amorous or both. There were some couples trying to create an illusion of romance in a bar where pint pitchers are being knocked back with the regularity of underage teens outside a club, and there were the same underage teens setting in motion the process that would see them get knocked back later on this evening. It wasn't as if this pub contained every element of Glasgow life, but it sure contained a lot of it.

After a further pint after their meal, the boys moved next door to MacSorleys. "Blooming hell, they've cleaned this place up a bit," said Terry. "Aye mate, new owners and a lot of work has gone into it" replied James, but Terry quickly replied, "Nah, not all that, I just mean that they've actually cleaned it, I'm not sure if that ever happened when we used to come here." The two guys laughed before they were bamboozled at the bar by a dazzling array of pints and bottles. It wasn't like this in the old days before settling on two pints of whatever was in the pump next to the barmaid.

As Terry sat and sipped his pint, he took the time to look around the venue. It was clearly the same place he used to come regularly, the same shape, and the memories were flooding back. However, it was a hugely different place and it had a different feel. Maybe this is what he needed, to see that he had moved on, but that other places and people had moved on too. You can certainly miss what is no longer around, but there is no point in pining for it anymore because there's nothing you can do to bring it back.

At the conclusion of the pint, Terry said, "Look mate, the music's getting a bit loud and I'm starting to worry about how young these lassies are! Annie got some beers in, fancy heading back to mine?"

James was quick to agree, and after a quick pit-stop, well, a medium length pit-stop, that is something that doesn't get any easier as you get older, the boys were heading home.

While not being steaming, the two were obviously in a chatty and gassy mood, making the bus journey fly by. As Terry made his way into the gate, he noticed the lights were on. "That daftie must have forgot to switch the lights off, I'll pull her up for wasting money when I see her" and he put the key in the door. After the third attempt.

He wiggled the key, the mechanism clicked, he stumbled inside and heard "SURPRISE!!!"

Terry then looked up and at the doorway to the living room, Annie was standing, kitted out in gear he had never seen her wear before. Terry made his way forward, and before he could speak, the sound system kicked into life, blaring out "The Passenger" by Iggy Pop. That was a shock, Annie had never shown any interest for that sort of music, but once he made his way to the living room, he was in for a bigger shock. Daft Shuggie, Jackie and Joe, even Mandy and that pal of hers he never remembered the name of.

"Bloody hell," said Terry, "I've not seen half of you lot since we last went to…." And it was then that it dawned on him as he looked at Annie.

"Terry helped me round them up, we thought you needed a wee bit of nostalgia and to say goodbye to it all, fancy a beer?"

As Annie grabbed a few beers from the fridge, James grabs Terry from the back, "awright mate, someone uploaded the final setlist from Optimo on the internet, I've got most of it…I don't think I've got it all in order, but we'll have a right good dance."

At times, they actually turned the music down so they could have a conversation, which certainly wouldn't have happened in the old days and a few folk had to nip off to get home to let the babysitter get away. It wasn't a like for like remake of the good old days, but it was better than anything Terry could have imagined. The brilliant music, the brilliant company, plenty of beer that was already paid for and a couch to sit back on, this was even better than Optimo!

It wasn't really Annie's sort of music, but every so often, a tune that she recognised would come on and she'd be up dancing. There'd also be a lot of funny or cool songs that she liked as well, "You know Terry, this stuff ain't too bad…well some of it" she said as Green Velvet kicked in, "some of it isn't for me honey!"

One by one, people started drifting away until it was Annie, Terry and James kicking about.
"You'd better turn the music off Terry, we don't want to piss the neighbours off too much" said Annie.

James piped up "Come on Terry, just one more tune, one more tune, one more tune, one more tune" to which Terry joined in with, and before too long, Annie was involved too.

"Aye, one more tune," said James, and as 'Losing My Edge' by LCD Soundsystem kicked in, he felt it was time to say goodbye. Losing his edge? Aye…but he had found another one….

I'm Hating On That Bam

Squelch.

3, 2, 1…

And there was the realisation that yet again, Martin Dorans had stood on dog droppings. No matter the term you used for the mess that dogs leave behind them, it doesn't make standing on it any more pleasant. The thing is though, it was turning out to be a regular occurrence for Martin. No matter if he was heading for the bus, popping to the local store, nipping out for a smoke or even going out for a run, Martin's street was becoming like an assault course with fresh traps waiting to catch out people who were not fully focused on the path stretching out in front of them.

Given that Martin was hardly the most attentive of chaps, it was fair to say that he was stepping in more than his fair share of dog's muck these days. Some people may say its muck for luck, but Martin's more natural reaction was of a different rhyme.

It didn't use to be this way. Budhill Avenue used to be a quiet street where you could walk up and down in a daydream and be absolutely untroubled. That all changed the day Billy Travers moved into Martin's close. The warning signs were ominous, the devil dog was tied up in the garden when Martin returned home from work and there were boxed strewn across the close. They laid there for days and then those days turned into weeks before the weeks turned into months. Thankfully the dog had been untied and retrieved from the front garden in that time, but there was no mistaking that Billy Travers was a man that made an impact.

Loud music. Drunk friends coming and going at all hours of the night and day. Arguments between him and his on-off girlfriend. These were common occurrences in the close, but of course, the most nagging problem was the multitude of dog droppings that were littering the street.

Posters were placed on lampposts reminding people that they had a duty to look after the local area, which meant that cleaning up after their dog was a mandatory task. These signs, in an enormous font and laminated to withstand the changeability of the Glasgow weather, had no impact. There was a question over whether Billy had noticed or indeed if Billy was able to read the sign, but there was one tell-tale sign that Billy had indeed stumbled across the signs.

This was when old Mrs McCarver from two houses down went for a Sunday morning walk only to find one of the posters ripped from the lamppost, lying on the ground with a doggy retort placed directly on it. It was clear that a simple poster campaign was not going to engineer a community spirit in Billy.

Phone calls were made to the council but they were unwilling to get involved. They didn't have the manpower and without any evidence, there was nothing that they could do to bring Billy to justice.

Even after Martin and a few other people promised to get evidence, the council said that the evidence would not be acceptable as it had come from people who had previously made a complaint and who could be viewed as to having a biased opinion against the person who was being complained about.

Martin thought what was the bloody point of it all and in a way, he was right. There was no way the council were going to get involved and it was hardly a matter that the police would be looking to resolve. After so many complaints of why weren't they out catching real criminals, it would have been a bit hypocritical for the residents of Budhill Avenue to start demanding that the local police force get their fingers out of their backside and catch a dog pooper in his tracks.

It was then that Martin decided that if anything was going to come of it, they would need to take action themselves. If the council and the law aren't going to help you, it's time to take the law into your own hands and Martin sought council over what he, and they, should do next.

"No Martin, that is possibly the stupidest idea of all time. Please don't do that."

It was not the ringing vote of confidence that Martin was looking for but to be honest, he didn't expect his idea to be a popular one at first but he was yet to make his plea on behalf of his idea. Martin spoke calmly and objectively to some other neighbours from the close in a specially convened meeting.

There had been talk of a neighbourhood watch scheme being set up in the light of the unpleasantness at No. 48 but that quickly fizzled out. Martin couldn't be bothered going through the rigmarole of organising an official gathering so he put a note through Jenny from upstairs door and he grabbed a word with Shug on his way out of the flat one morning. Three was the magic number and a number that Martin believed would be more than enough to put his plan into action.

The first refusal for the idea came from Jenny and it was a more measured response than the one delivered by Shug.

"Have you gone off your nut wee man?"

With hindsight, the notion of poisoning the dog was an outrageous one but Martin quickly followed up by saying that he didn't want to kill the dog, he just wanted to…well, he didn't really know what he wanted to do. He certainly wanted to give Billy a fright and the thought of the dog having a dodgy stomach and doing his mess all over Billy's house was certainly a humorous one.

Jenny interjected "But Martin, if you make the dog unwell, his mess on the street is likely to be in that condition as well. That will be even worse."

Which was a fair point thought Martin as he shrugged.

"Anyway ya daftie, it's not the dugs fault, it's that big arsehole that owns the dug that is the problem, can we not poison him?" asked Shug.

Ordinarily, the notion of poisoning a man is not one that people would be in favour of. Pranks and gags are all well and good but taking the steps to poison someone to the point of illness or perhaps even more was a step away from what would be considered good behaviour in the big society.

It was an appalling suggestion, one that had Martin and Jenny shaking their heads instantly and Shug's face started to contort in a way that it hadn't done since that time he had been caught peeing in the school swimming pool by the PE Teacher. Shug certainly wasn't the first boy to pee into the Hillpark pool but given that he was standing outside of the pool at the time, his situation was a little bit different. Like then, he was about to apologise but found that his words had been blocked off by other people. At school, it was the bellowing of his teacher, which saw Shug eventually be suspended for 3 days. Here, it was the softly spoken words of Martin.

"Aye, I'm in."

"Me too" added Jenny and before you know it, plans were being made to take the big man down. Martin had access to poison at work, rat killer and the like, enough to make a bit of a dent in someone. Martin was tasked with finding out the dosage of what it would take to make someone feel rather unwell but not kill them or make their vital organs shut down. As the old saying goes "sticking poison onto other people's food is all fun and games until someone gets violently ill or loses their sight".

Shug was the surveillance man. He had earned this title through 15 years of hard work and dedication of being a nosey bastard. If you wanted to know the gossip on anyone in the street, Shug knew the ins, the outs and all the whys and wherefores. He knew when Billy left the house and he probably knew the routine and route better than Billy knew it himself.

Every day at 12:17, no doubt just after Billy waved bye bye to Holly Willoughby for another day, he grabs his dug and marches him down the street. He pops into the local bakery and buys two pies before heading into the local park. There, he places his paper on a bench, places his pies on the paper and then goes to the van for some juice before returning to devour the lot, including the tabloid tittle tattle in the Star. Billy used to read the Record and the Sun but found the Record has become too preachy for his liking and the Sun has become a little bit too highbrow.

Given Billy's wide state, once his back was turned on his paper and rolls as he made his way to the van, there was a good few moments worth of opportunity to impact on the pies. There were tankers turning in the North Sea at a faster rate than Billy could manage, and this was the opportunity for an extra special seasoning to be added to the convivial blend of grease, rock hard pastry and mechanically retrieved assorted meat.

Jenny's role was…well, Jenny wasn't going to do much but Martin and Shug wanted another set of fingerprints on it just in case. Martin would likely be the one that would sprinkle the poison on the pies but Jenny was going to hang around just in case a decoy was needed. The plan was set – Martin would get the poison before the weekend and then spend the weekend researching and getting the measurements right and then Monday would be the day of reckoning.

On Sunday night, Martin felt like a child on the night before Christmas. He knew it was a horrible thing he was about to do but it is not as if he was going to kill or seriously injure Billy, hopefully just give him enough gut rot to keep him laying low for a week. Ironically given that he was setting out to do ill-will on someone in his close, the sense of community spirit he was sharing with Shug and Jenny had Martin positively brimming with glee. An hour of counting sheep did nothing for Martin but eventually, counting the falling Billy's in the park soon saw Martin fall under the spell of the sandman.

At midday, Martin left the house and made his way to the park. He would position himself down from the row of benches, obscured from sight by trees and unkempt hedges. This would be enough time to get him from his hiding spot to the pies and back in the amount of time that Billy took to trek to the van and back.

Billy text Jenny "the fox is in the hole" to which Jenny replied, "that poor fox, I hope you help him out before Billy gets there." Jenny was a pretty girl but she was dumb and dull thought Martin, maybe he'd ask her out one day.

Shug was hovering at his living room window, which was nothing out of the ordinary from him. In the background buzz and hum of the room, he ascertained that This Morning was finishing up and within a minute or two, as right as rain, Billy was stoating out on the pavement, devil dog yapping at the bit and being hauled back by Billy's slow pace.

Squeezing up against his window and squinting, Shug saw Billy make his way to bakery and then come out with the usual bag. This was the limit of Shug's work and he text Martin, "Billy's got his pies, with you shortly".

So Martin waited.

And waited.

And waited.

He then ate an apple he had in his pocket but then he waited some more.

Eventually his phone buzzed, it was a text from Jenny "you had better come back to the main road".
Martin made his way out of the park, around the corner and stopped in front of the ambulance. Hold on, that isn't usually there during the day. He heard a barking sound and there was Jenny holding onto the devil dog of Billy's.

"Things didn't quite go to plan Martin" said Jenny.

Shug was right that Billy did go into the bakery and snapped up two pies before making his way towards the park. For whatever reason, the bag containing the pies was so sodden with grease that the flimsy paper disintegrated less than 10 yards outside of the shop. In the blink of an eye, the two pies were hurtling towards the ground faster than you could say Glasgow was the sick man of Europe.

At moments like this, your life can flash before your eyes and then instinct kicks in. Billy let go of the dog leash and lurched forward to save his pies from a fate worse than death, a manky Glaswegian pavement. Billy was fast but his dog was faster and in one fell swoop, caught the first pie in his mouth and was tearing into it with abandon.

Billy landed with a thud and by the time his head picked itself up from the ground, the first pie was gone and the second one didn't have long for this earth.

"Ya wee bassa, I'll throttle you" screamed Billy and reached out an arm for his dog, grabbing its hindleg. Billy's fingers were slippy from the pie grease on the bag though, allowing his dog to slip from his grasp, which was all the opportunity the dog needed to scoop the pie into its mouth.

Billy clamoured to his feet and again roared at his dog "I'll murder ye" and aimed a kick at an animal that was being anything but man's best friend. No doubt realising that now was not a opportune time to hang around, the dog leapt into the middle of the road to where Billy followed him, picking up a head of steam. It was here that Billy's inability to turn saw him come a cropper. His dog, as quickly as it jumped onto the road managed to jump back to the safety of the pavement, leaving Billy to face a double decker bus head on.

It looked an even contest but the pace of the bus was the telling factor, knocking Billy out and causing a whole heap of commotion on the bus.

"Oh for fuck sake driver, I've got to sign on in ten minutes, I'm gonna be late…just go round the fat bassa" was one rather unhelpful comment but as you can imagine, the driver was rather shook up about what had just transpired. That and he probably got a touch of whiplash from when the bus bounced off Billy.

A dozen or so calls were made to the emergency services and one or two were made to the city council informing them of a hole in the road that needed to be fixed.

Before too long, the ambulance appeared and with the assistance of the police, Billy was lifted into the back of the ambulance. He was awake and mumbling. "You'll be awright son, just lie back" was the advice of the ambulance assistant and Billy whispered back, "Where's my dug?"

It was a natural reaction, most people on receiving a shock like that would first of all ask about their loved ones. The ambulance assistant responded that Billy's dog was fine and that Billy could see him later. "I'll bloody kill him when I see him" Billy intoned and then shut his eyes and mouth again.

Jenny had seen it all and was in a state of shock. She explained the story to the police and they were calling out someone from the RSPCA to take a hold of the dog for now. Jenny was holding onto him for safe keeping but filled with the greasy goodness of two pies and outwitting his particularly dumb owner, the dog was looking rather content with life.

"I'll see you later then" said Martin as Jenny hung around, and on his way back to the flat, he placed the vial of poison into one of the bins and vowed to chalk this one up to experience.

Farmfood's Al

You know what it is like with some couples. They just seem destined to be together and even though they spend most of their formative years apart trying out other relationships, you just know that in the end, they'll come to their senses and shack up together. Perhaps this is the hopelessly romantic outlook on life or maybe it is the way that Hollywood and TV executives have conditioned us to think but sometimes when a couple are so right for each other, you get the feeling that the whole nation is rooting for them to be together.

Plans can change though with unforeseen events getting in the way. The third party that gets in the way of a perfect couple is occasionally hounded, and the weight of public opinion can drive them away, bringing the main protagonists back to their senses and giving people the happy ending they were looking for. Sometimes though, sometimes the third party is strong enough to take the flak, the hate, the criticism and keep on coming back for more before eventually the public is won over and the new couple is eventually accepted by all and sundry.

This was how it was in Glasgow in 2011 when Greggs and Iceland released a statement that they were hooking up with Iceland stocking frozen Greggs products in all of their stores. There was delight at the thought of never having to leave your home (after the initial purchase) to get a Greggs again but there was outrage too. This wasn't a tie-up deal that was meant for Iceland, the good people of Glasgow already had Farmfoods in their heart and this was where Greggs should have ended up. The cold embrace of a Farmfoods freezer cabinet would have been the perfect resting place for Greggs to lay down their sausage rolls and their chilli steak lattices but the dream of watching these companies come together and help us grow to middle age in poor health and with clogged arteries were being ripped asunder by the intervention of Iceland.

It is not as though Iceland was overly popular in Glasgow anyway. A lot of people remembered the shop when it was Bejam and why would you ever want to change from a name that was as cool as Bejam? It was almost as though Iceland was running away from its past, desperate to create a new identity but this new relationship seemed to bring all these old memories to the fore. There was also that televised incident with the Glaswegian bam bellowing "I hate Iceland" in an airport. Okay, that was aimed at the country for not properly controlling their volcanoes, but when the tie-in was announced, the screams of "I hate Iceland" were heard throughout the city.

In the end though, the furore died down and like you should do in times of trouble, people followed the pastries. Of course, Farmfoods was an integral part of everyday life for so many people but with Iceland featuring much of the similar stock and having the Greggs seal of approval, it was too hard to ignore. Little by little, resistance to Iceland faded away, Greggs were making the sort of money that only a disgraced banker would be comfortable with making and Farmfoods was looked upon with a pitying empathy, the sort usually reserved for spinster aunts and ill dogs. Iceland had won and they were not slow in flaunting it, releasing new Greggs products with impunity every few months. Greggs was still doing a roaring trade, Iceland weren't touching on the passing customers, the lunch-time trade or the continually changing cakes related to the time of year trade but when it came to the dinner and night-time snacks market, Iceland hadn't just won the battle; they had triumphed in the war with consummate ease. Given the state of some of the own brand produce created by both companies, there could have been chemical warfare and dirty bombs activities if it came to a war but there was little appetite for the fight at Farmfoods HQ. With Greggs on the other side, it was a losing battle, one that had the PR winner and the physical artillery firmly camped with the opposition.

The famous quote that an army marches on its stomach is attributed to Napoleon Bonaparte and he was right but in Glasgow, the population marches to and on Greggs, Farmfoods couldn't compete with that. Except for one part of the city, where the employees of one store had no intention of giving up the fight. In the leafy West End suburbs, there was no acknowledgment of the split that had affected the rest of Glasgow but in Shawlands, there was a lot to play for.

The Shawlands Arcade has seen better days, it has seen a lot of better days but the Farmfoods store had developed a reputation of being a fun place to shop. This reputation may owe something to the proximity to death's waiting room ambience that can be found in the Victoria Road Farmfoods but a lot of the popularity lay in the staff at the Shawlands Arcade store. It is easy to have people looking down their noses at certain jobs in the retail market but in the current climate, a job's a job and more often than not, a job is what you make it. Store manager Al Jardine was a great believer in giving out happy vibes and this was part of the daily process for the employees. The heavy shutters were rolled up at 9am but at 8.50, the early morning staff would gather around the tills, close to the chocolates and mints, sing a 60s pop song and then shout out one thing that they are happy with in their life. It was cheesy, it was naff, it was all the things that the cool people would roll their eyes at but when you're working in a shop selling freezer produce, you don't need to worry about being cool; you were already cooler than cool!

It sounded silly but this upbeat behaviour definitely made its way into the interaction the employees had with the customers. With a focus on frozen food, it would be understandable that most customers would come once a week tops, perhaps fortnightly or monthly but the expansion of the store had opened up a market for the popping in brigade.

Bread, milk, eggs, sugar, biscuits and juice were all available at rock bottom prices, and the regular faces were soon known on first name terms by the staff. There was Elsie Jones, the mum of three who would drop the kids off at school and then pop into Farmfoods for the daily essentials. Tommy and Sadie Wylie, a married couple of 47 years (with 34 happy years) who took in the store on their daily walk. Jimmy Gibbs, picking up milk and crisps for the boys in the work van every morning. Even the school kids were a regular feature, a 3 pack of Toblerone and 3 cans of pop for a pound providing a cheap lunch and leaving money aside for buying single cigarettes or whatever youngsters were into these days. There was a community feel to the store but one by one, the lure of the Greggs deal started eroding the customer base from the shop and the familiar faces become less familiar.

It would have been easy to take this on the chin and accept their fate but this was not the way Al Jardine rolled. He had been on to head office looking for support to try a few promotions to bring the punters back and was fully expecting to be told this was not on. Surprisingly, Al was given free reign. Okay, the exact wording was "do what you want, it's over, grab what you can and get out, they've killed us man…they've killed us" followed by quite a lot of sobbing but reading between the lines, Al believed this was the commercial freedom he was looking for. There were going to be some changes around here thought Al, starting from this weekend.

It was the height of summer and plenty of folk were arranging BBQs. This usually meant heading to the local supermarket to ransack the drinks aisles and then grab some food and buns on the way to the till but Farmfoods was picking up some residual customers. Lets face it, you were getting 96 burgers for a £1, throw in some buns, juice and ice cream, and you could feed the entire street while pocketing enough change from a fiver to get a quick pint in the Wetherspoons on the way home.

If people wanted BBQs, Al decided to give them a BBQ. At the front of the store, Al set up one of those store bought BBQs and made up a sign. FREE HOT DOG FOR EVERY PAYING CUSTOMER. He took some hot dogs that were getting perilously close to their sell-by date (Al declined to say if they were close to being out of date or if they were perilously close to being in date), some onions and got a whip round from the staff members to pay for the buns. This went down as well as you would expect it to but once Al outlined the neediness of the situation, it was hard to say no.

"Look, if this place goes under, we all lose our jobs and that means no money coming in. If these hot dogs keep folk coming into the store, it's a pound off your wage, WHICH WILL STILL BE A LOT BETTER THAN NO BLOODY WAGE AT ALL!!"

That was more than enough to rally the troops and there was no shortage of volunteers to man the BBQ. It was a whole lot better than being sat on the till or mucking about in the stock room. Word started to spread as twitter and facebook came alive with the sound of free barely edible hotdogs. The southsiders of Glasgow know all about value and a path was being beaten to the store. Some customers were coming in and filling baskets and trollies, taking advantage of the low prices and then getting some free food at the end of it. The smarter shopper was going in to the store, buying one item, enjoying a hot dog and then going back in and repeating the purchase. A free hot dog with every purchase means a free hot dog with every purchase. One fly swine who spent £5 on five different items, putting each one through as a single transaction, helped himself to five free hot dogs while the wee woman who spent a tenner on messages in one go was only entitled to one hot dog.

Thems the breaks and it just shows how far you can go when you beat the system. Al was annoyed at this; he thought it was playing the system when there was absolutely no need to. It was only a bloody Farmfoods hot dog!

Near the end of the day, they decided to call a halt and gave the hot dogs away in one free bundle. The staff closed up shop and Al did the sums. Even allowing for the additional outlay, the extra wage of having a staff member standing outside as opposed to stock-taking and giving all the staff members their pound for the buns back, the shop had made a profit. A big profit. In fact, it was the biggest days takings the shop had since Thatcher died and party food was flying off the shelves. Al couldn't rely on a despised political figure dying every week to bring the money in to the store but perhaps he could rely on a great summer with BBQ promotions running every week.

He couldn't, mainly because the weather was rubbish and secondly because all the people who tasted the hot dogs were in no rush to come back the following week for another round. Undeterred, Al didn't stop there but no matter what he did, he was thwarted, blocked or failed to offer an enticing incentive for his customers.

He promised to provide a free newspaper to pre 10am customers who bought something but with the Metro being handed out just down from the store, there was no rush of people beating a path to the store to get their tabloid fix. He toyed with the idea of having a fancy dress day where every customer in fancy dress got a free carton of eggs (nearing their sell-by date). This was until he looked out of his office and noticed that everyone in the store was wearing what could be passed off as fancy dress. The guy in a yellow shellsuit was close to looking like Ali G. The dull schoolboy with uniform and glasses looked like the briefcase wanker from the Inbetweeners. Bloody hell, even that woman was dressed as a sexy nurse…no wait, she genuinely was an attractive lady in her works uniform but still, who was to say what was fancy dress or not?

All it needed was one big idea, something to bring the punters in and get loads of publicity. How hard can it be to find inspiration, its Glasgow, the most creative city in the world. It was then that Al thought it was best to sit back and let the idea come to him. When you chase inspiration, it goes hiding but when you turn your back on it, it appears at your window, rapping on the pane, waking up the neighbourhood.

The next moment, the phone rang waking Al from his daydream of an idea going about battering windows and he thought to himself, this will be it, this is the big moment.

It was.

"Al, you've fought the good fight but it's over, we're selling up all the south of Glasgow stores, we're struggling big time over there, the store will run for 6 more weeks but after that, it's finished. Someone from HR will be out during the week to speak to staff."

Al was struck dumb and didn't know what to say. He knew he had to tell the staff but how…not now…let him come to terms with it first and then tell everyone tomorrow. And with that, the office door was being rattled, "come in" shouted Al.

In stormed two of the checkout girls, "whats this that all of the Glasgow shops are closing?"

Bloody hell thought Al, good news travels fast round here. "Where did you hear that?"

"I just got a text from Debs that works over in Vicky Road, aw the Glasgow shops are shutting, we'll be out in 6 weeks."

The look on Al's face hopefully said it all but perhaps the two girls were not adept at reading….faces….I better say something thought Al. "Sadly yes, it's true, I just took the phone call, I was planning on telling you all at the end of the shift. Sorry"

"Debs said they've all walked out on strike, the shops being raided as we speak by the locals, they'll be nothing left."

Madness thought Al, utter madness. "Look girls, I know folk will be pissed off, I am too, I'll lose my job like everyone else. The thing is though, we've got six weeks more pay to get if we stick in, the Vicky Road staff are going to get nothing…it's not worth it. That and if they're sacked, they have to wait before signing on."

That was the clincher, "aye boss, we'll get back to work".

News spread around colleagues fast, but it wasn't too long before it spread around the local community. Regular shoppers were popping in and saying their goodbyes and passing on their condolences. There was another person though who made his way to the manager's office and it took a few seconds for Al to place him and then it clicked, I know that smarmy bassa, its….

"Tom Jackson, general manager of Iceland in Scotland. We've heard a lot of positive things about you Al and we'd like to offer you a job. The Iceland down the road is the one with the poorest takings in Glasgow and we think it's down to the work you guys are doing here. We want you to be our new store manager down the road."

Wow. As opportunities go, there's one you need to let it sink in. All the while Al was fighting for the store, little did he know that he was putting out his own CV. Sometimes it's the things you do when you don't realise what you're doing that matter the most. "That's an amazing offer, I'd love to" said Al but (and there is always a but), "only if I can bring my team members."

Tom looked at Al as if Al said he'd only take the job if he got a jump on Tom's wife and daughter.

"Are you mad Al? You know and I know this store is going under, this is your way out, don't let yourself be dragged under with the wreckage. I'll leave it with you" and with that, Mr Jackson upped and left.

As soon as the door was closed, Al's head fell instantly on to the desk, the weight of the problem vastly outweighing gravity and the regular mode of behaviour. It would be madness for Al not to take the job, in the current job climate; you can't turn down an offer like that? With a mortgage to pay off and a Sky Sports subscription to keep up, Al couldn't afford to lose this job but could he let everyone down by betraying them?

He couldn't but he had to. That night, Al got no sleep at all but he knew for once that he had to do the right thing for himself. The team were good people, they'd bounce back, he'd give everyone a glowing reference, he'd even print off all of their CVs and covering letters on the office printer before he finished up, it wouldn't be pretty but he had to do it.

As he made his way to the store, Al was all over the shot. He didn't like the thought of letting people down but he knew he was doing right for himself. He picked up a Metro at the foot of the arcade, folded it under his arm and made his way in to the store. There were a few messages on the answer machine, brilliant thought Al, more sickies. He couldn't blame staff members; it was hard to keep the enthusiasm and motivation up. He clicked on the phone and started to listen.

"Al have you seen the news, great news" was message one.

"Message for Al Jardine, this is head office, a delegation of directors will be at the store at 10am, please be ready" was message two.

"Brilliant gaffer, we're saved" said the third and final message.

Al pinched himself to make sure he wasn't dreaming. He wasn't but now he was still confused and had a sore arm that would likely bruise in a day or two. Unfolding his newspaper, the front page read

ICE TEAM WARS!

It was a clever Glasgow related pun on the looting of the Vicky Road store, but as Al paid attention to the text and not the cheesy headline, he realised that there was a lot more to it. Farmfoods bosses had decided to close the Vicky Road branch down early due to the strike and looting but they also detailed that they were going to keep the other Glasgow stores open. Analysis of the impact that the lost days takings and stock losses at the Victoria Road store placed a new light on the Glasgow's stores takings and profits. The company reviewed city areas collectively as opposed to individual stores and it turns out that the Victoria Road store was a huge drain on resources and profits. All of the other Glasgow stores were doing well and the Shawlands Arcade one was doing a roaring trade.

The directors were coming over to say that they were putting a new focus behind the remaining south of Glasgow stores and were going to put Al in charge of all of the local stores. Al was shocked, not at the goings on in the other store, how that was failing to make a profit was a massive question but at this, the thought of the good guys winning, that wasn't the way it was supposed to be in life.

The directors seemed shocked at the early morning sing song and pep rally but if it was working, they wanted it to work elsewhere. They may not have had Greggs to entice folk in with, but with Al, Farmfoods was on to a winner.

Venus In Firhill

"Right son, I'll get you outside at half-two, mind and be on time."

The tone of his dad's voice meant that Jackie knew that no was not going to be accepted as an answer. Every year the same rigmarole was played out and the same song and dance ensued. The few weeks off during the summer were bliss, allowing Jackie the freedom to do as he pleased and this time provided him with comfort knowing that he wasn't letting his dad down. As dads went, James Jack McPherson was a pretty decent one by Glasgow standards but there was one major flaw in his and his son's relationship. As you grow older, the distance that grows between yourself and your dad becomes quite painful, a realisation that your childhood is over, and your role model doesn't always do the things that you want him to do.

In Jackie's mind, the weekend was for freedom, for roaming the country in pursuit of new delights and for sleeping long in the afternoons in celebration and recovery from the excesses of the night before. We work hard enough in the Monday to Friday slog, to deny yourself pleasure and entertainment at the weekend is surely one of the most perverse activities that man has pursued. Tell it to James though, and Jackie had told him at various points in the weeks, months and even years leading to this date. At this point, James felt that this would be the day when he stood up to his dad and said "NO, I'm making my own decisions" but come half past two, he knew exactly where he would be.

"Awright dad, here we go again eh" said Jackie, shoulders permanently shrugged at what lay in store. His downbeat nature stood in opposition to the striding and forceful nature of his father, "Here we go again son but trust me, it's going to be a bit different this time, I can feel it." "You feel that every time dad, every time" was the too quick response from Jackie, almost barking back at his dad but nothing was going to demolish the upbeat nature of his dad….not today, it was the first day of the season and Firhill was glistening in the hazy Glasgow sunshine.

"We've made a couple of smart signings son" started James before extolling the virtues of the Bosmans, hopefuls and never-gonna-bes that had been snapped up by the management team. It seemed that not even the optimism of a new season could help Jackie rekindle that spark for Thistle that he had as a kid, he was afraid to say it but it had been beaten out of him. In football, consistency is seen as an admirable thing but not for Thistle. Consistency for Thistle means that they have found their place at a lower level, the true joy at Firhill came in those glorious yo-yo years. From destroying the opposition one season to clinging on for dear life the next season, never knowing where you stood with Thistle made Jackie feel alive. Sadly, he felt he knew exactly what was coming this season…a season of mid-table comfort and a cup quarter final at best.

When his dad and uncles talk of the 71 Cup final, a smile inevitably flickers across his face and in his eyes but the seasons where you never knew where you would end up were the greatest in Jackie's lifetime. This season, even before a ball had been kicked, Thistle looked too far good for the relegation zone but not strong enough to challenge for the promotion places. Another steady season awaited with the only hope of excitement or change resting on the cups, which was not the sort of thing Jackie could muster much enthusiasm for.

Tell that to Jackie's dad though, all the while Jackie had been meandering through his own back pages, James was rattling through the reasons why this year was going to be different. The management team knew the league now; they had the experience to get through it. The couple of old heads they picked up for free from the SPL would settle the club down, and the youngsters packed into midfield and up front would run the legs off all of the other donkeys finding sanctuary in the back fours and fives of the Scottish Football League. James was not just hoping for promotion, he was expecting it, this was to be the season Thistle would clinch a place back amongst the big boys.

After all, the Harry Wraggs were the second biggest team in the city and Glasgow needed two teams in the top flight. Edinburgh had two teams in the top flight and that's not even a proper city with good people. James was happy with the two Dundee teams being in the top flight, a proper derby he was prone to say and of course, the Highlands were well represented with Caley and Ross County battling out to be the best of the North and to avoid relegation. If the bloody Highlands could get two teams in the top flight, Glasgow needed to get its finger out and this was where Thistle would come in…"it is destiny son" was when Jackie clicked back into his dad's conversation, whereupon he managed to offer a weak smile in acknowledgment.

Destiny thought Jackie, crikey, there was a club that was worse than Thistle! To be fair though, there are a lot of bad clubs in Glasgow and Partick Thistle are nowhere near the worst of them. If you're in Maryhill and want to check out the worst club, get yourself along to Framptons and see how the night pans out. "Jackie son, this season is going to be better trust me…right, get the pies and bovrils in before the teams come out, here's a tenner."

It was probably the sunniest day of the year and Jackie would spend a great part of the game sitting with his hand perched in front of his face to block out the sun and here he was going to get two pies and two Bovrils…that is the power of tradition for you. Mind you, on a day like this you are looking for a cold drink and some chilled food so a Firhill

Bovril and pie was probably the ideal accompaniment to the great Glasgow sunshine.

Ten to three and no queue at the pie-stall, a cracking result in a way but a poor one for the money men and lassies at the club. It's not as if Thistle are going to make a bomb from their catering output but even on minimum wages, the staff need to get paid, suppliers need their money and electricity needs to be accounted for before the club starts making a profit on the catering. The food and drink purchase was less out of necessity, more out of the drive to keep the club going. If Armageddon was rolling into Scottish football, Jackie wonders if we would even notice the difference…perhaps the pies might be hotter!

Walking to the front of the kiosk, Jackie was astounded by what he saw. The notion of a low fat Scotch pie (technically lower fat would be the proper title) was shocking enough but behind the counter, rather than a plukey faced teenager staring gormlessly into space (much like Thistle's left back of the previous season) stood a rather fetching young lady. Even with the polyester look of a football catering uniform to contend with, this girl was the best thing that Jackie had seen inside Firhill for about three years.

"How can I help you sir?" beamed the young girl with Mary on her name tag, "There's some new options for this season so if you need any recommendations, please just ask." Service with a smile in football stadium? Jackie had half a mind to turn around and walk back into the stand and come out again. This wasn't the way that things were meant to be thought Jackie…."Just two pies and two Bovrils please Mary."

"Not a problem sir" and off she popped. The fact that she first of all went for the Bovril order, applying the hot water to the pre-made up cartons was a change from the usual. It was fairly common for Jackie to be handed the pies immediately and then wait five minutes for the staff to get to grips with the urn and complete the Bovril order. A scolding hot drink could possibly balance out the now lukewarm pie, but no, here was customer service the way it was supposed to be. Even the price was calculated in the blink of an eye with the correct change delivered first time. Never mind what would unfold on the pitch during the game, this alone had been a revelation on the opening day of the season.

Taking his seat and handing over the food and drink to his dad, Jackie was still reeling. You're never going to believe this dad, they've actually got a pie shop worker that knows what they're doing he said. No waiting, correct change, she was even pleasant and polite." "A she eh…" and a raised eyebrow was all the reply that James had to muster but before Jackie could take the huff, Thistle were running out onto the lush grass you only get for the season opener and things were all set to get underway in Firhill.

Maybe it was the beefy goodness that was circulating through Jackie's body, maybe it was the mild sun burn he was experiencing as the Jackie Husband stand basked in the bright sunshine, but Thistle were looking a different proposition from the season before.

Much like his dad had said, there was a sturdiness at the back and the forward play was springing forward with gusto and invention. By half-time, Thistle were two goals to the good and it was only their own profligacy and some desperate defending that stopped the score-line being bigger. No one was stupid enough to get carried away on the back of a strong forty-five minutes, after all, this could be as good as things get for the Jags all season but you have to be happy with what you have at times.

The second half came and went with a slower pace, it would have been unlikely for the team to have kept going at the same pace and tenacity for the second 45 but the most impressive thing was, Thistle never let their dominance slip. At no point at all did they look as though they would surrender a goal. Football and especially football in Firhill doesn't work like that but with a clean sheet and 2 goals to celebrate, the season had gotten off to a great start in Maryhill.

As James and Jackie trooped out of the stadium, some fans arcing onto Maryhill Road, perhaps tempted by Munns Vaults, The Strathmore Bar or even with the wider delights of Byres Road, others dropping downwards into town in the direction of Great Western Road, James said; "I've got the car son if you want a lift?" It was a nice offer but you don't often get days like this in Glasgow and Jackie was determined to make the most of it. "No thanks dad, it's a nice day, I'll just walk back into town…I'll see you in midweek though" and as Jackie waved his dad off, the standard "call your mother" comment was delivered by his dad. Regular as clockwork, you never get a goodbye without reminding you to call your mammy…today had definitely been a good day.

Down Maryhill Road, past St Georges Cross and beyond the cavalcade of lights, fly-overs and the M8. Sure, it was no Autobahn, but this part of town had always seemed a bit other worldly to Jackie.

Now that he grown up he realised it was other worldly in that rubbish futuristic 1970s sense, but it was still a favourite part of town. It was the cut-off point between his Thistle life and his normal life. The top end of Sauchiehall Street is such a hive of nonsense, shenanigans and excessive drinking, it was almost made to transport you away from Firhill and into another dimension.

Mind you, if the unfinished motorway flyovers and carbuncle shite-holes of Charing Cross weren't 70s enough for you, the Variety finished the job. Every single time you step through the doors was a step-back in time, albeit a particularly pleasant one. Great tunes, a great range of drinks and normally great company meant that this was the place to be and unsurprisingly, the boys were already here. Rather than spending Saturday afternoon at the football, Tony, Micky and Cass opted for the happiness of the bookies and Soccer Saturday.

"What's the scores on the doors lads?" enquired Jackie, knowing that tales of bad luck, late goals and downright vile refereeing decisions would have hampered the get rich scheme of the three diddies that stood before him.

"Very well Jackmeister very well, I am currently £86 better off and it is all thanks to a last minute equaliser by Scunthorpe. I only pick them because they have a very rude word in their name and there you go, over 80 bangers. These clowns, trying to pick the winners through football knowledge and in-depth analysis of the form. I told them, there's no form book for the first day of the season…but would they listen? So me and you can get absolutely Scunthorped in the next few rounds and these losers can watch on…hopefully it will give them the incentive to get better with their bets."

"Don't be a dick Tony, get us a beer" pleaded Micky, no doubt knowing he would have to stretch his money out for the next few hours unless the late kick-off did him a favour or he got lucky on the puggies. The beaming smile on Tony's face suggested that all would be well; "two rounds I'm getting in you swines and then we're back on an even keel, if I can slip some money back to the good lady, I'll be in the good books and you all know what that means on a Saturday night" and just as Tony was starting to make a rude gesture, Cass piped up; "Aye, you'll get to see the start of Match Of The Day before you fall asleep and then the missus will belt you for falling asleep on the couch yet again."

With his number being called perfectly by Cass, Tony got the beers in.

"That's the thing boys; it's just further bad luck for you that it's me who has got the lucky touch. If it was your main man Jackie here, you'd be in line for a windfall, it is not as if he has to take any of his winnings back home to the wife is it?" It was a fair point, wrapped in an insult, the sort that only a good mate could deliver. "Shut up ya dick…you know that Tracey was being an utter cow and then I had my exams…I'll get back on it soon enough and then I'll not spending my Saturday evenings with you bawbags" snapped Jackie.

The stereotypical "ooooohhhh" response was cut off by Tony, rising to the bait, "look Jacks, with studying and the Thistle, where are you going to be meeting a lassie? At Firhill…cos I'd like to see the lassie you'd bring from there."

On an ordinary day, this sort of jibe would be dismissed but today, on the first day of the season when the Jags stamped their class on every blade of grass of the pitch, Jackie was in no mood for Tony's snash. "I'll let you know there was a cracking lassie at Firhill today, pie stall lassie, wee darlin' so she was." Even the music in the Variety seemed to stop to make the laughter seem louder…

"Aye, I bet you were interested in the pie ya dirty bastard" cackled Tony into his Tennents…"what age was she if she was working at the fitba…you better watch yourself Jackie boy or the only team you'll be seeing this season is Peterhead." Another round of laughter, with twice the volume and intensity of the last, rolled around the booth with a barman shooting over a look to say "simmer down lads", heads were dipped but pint tumblers were raised in acknowledgment as the laughter at Jackie continued with restricted giggles. The night turned out to be another fun but ultimately uneventful night as beer and the ever impending football highlights on the telly took their toll.

Over the next few weeks, something strange happened in Glasgow, Partick Thistle kept on winning.

The weather was as unpredictable as ever, the buses were blithely ignoring any notion of a timetable but on the park, Thistle were turning up the odds, rewriting the form book and actually finding some consistency in their football. It wasn't always pretty, it wasn't always thrilling but when you're winning, you can overlook the slight negatives by looking at the bigger picture. Off the park, Firhill was a happier place to be, the grass behind the town-side goal may have been as unkempt as Jackie's hair but people were turning up in greater numbers with every passing win and the catering stalls were providing the sort of winning run that was equal to the first team.

Jackie's dad was supposed to be watching his weight and food intake, there was nothing seriously wrong with him, he was just a Glaswegian male past the prime of his life, but doctors' orders aren't as important as a winning football team. There are many things which influence the outcome of a football match, tactics, training, better players, rubbish refs and luck but above them all, there is something that some fans prize above all of the other factors involved in the game. Superstition.

Yes, as much as you pin your hopes on the centre-forward doing his job, it doesn't really matter what he does because the entire outcome of the match depends on the pants the guy in Row L Seat 48 is wearing. Or at least that's what the nutter in Row L Seat 48 thinks. James McPherson wasn't so crazy to think that his underpants could influence the outcome of a Thistle match, not after that season he nearly bankrupted himself buying new pants after every loss but he was a firm believer in keeping things the same around the match. James and Jackie had to meet half an hour before kick-off, he had to grab a programme, he had to put his scarf on second after kick-off, and of course, a factor in the opening win of the season was the pies and Bovrils, so these had to be part of the match day experience every game.

Jackie would sigh at his dad's reminder to head down and get the food order, but of course, he was delighted. He would get the chance to see the lassie working in the pie stall and hopefully unleash those lines he had been working on during the week.

"Steak? No thinks love, I've already put a bet on."

"Two pies? No, it's all my own hair."

"Would you look at that, I've not seen as much as grease since my mum went through her John Travolta phrase."

Yes, all of these lines were absolutely terrible but Scottish league football and lukewarm catering hardly provides you the best opportunities to chat up a girl and it was the best that Jackie could come up. The right line or situation never came up to unleash any of these lines, thankfully but week by week, he managed to have some chat with the young girl and then Thistle would eke out another win. Things were going brilliantly and by the time Raith Rovers came to town, the Jags were clear at the top of the league and looking as though this could be the year. There had been some tricky games on the run so far, games where the usual Thistle would have succumbed to a silly defeat or a morale bursting desperate draw but this time, it was going right and as you would expect, James McPherson was proud of his role in the starring run.

Just before kick-off, the usual song and dance of James telling his son to go and get the pies in was played out but with attendances on the up, there was a queue in front of Jackie by the time he bounded down to the kiosk. Standing behind a loud-mouth and his mate, Jackie seemed irked at the delay but no doubt more concerned about the chat that was unfolding in front of him. "Awright darling, gies a couple of pies and hows about I take you out on the town tonight?"

This alone was a blow to the heart of James. Here, he was playing the long game, the tika-taka continual pass and move stuff associated with Barcelona and the Spanish team. The trick is to keep plugging away until the right chance comes along and then you move in for the kill with a gilt-edged opportunity. Patience and niceties are not for every team and every one though and Jackie was appalled that this route one approach had got to a stage where he still seemed weeks, if not months, away from. Much like a kiosk crowd eagerly listening in to the question of "are they pies hot?" Jackie was straining forward waiting to hearing the response. "Two pies sir, not a problem…and I'm sorry, I won't be able to hit the town with you."

Phew….the chance had been kicked off the line, but before Jackie had the chance to celebrate, the follow up line of "it's against club policy for employees to date fans or customers. If you went and supported another team and never came back to Firhill, you could ask again. Thanks."

Match abandoned thought Jackie.

These words ripped through Jackie's heart like an overlapping full-back darting into space and before the fan in front could collect his pies, Jackie had feigned a ringing phone in his pocket and sloped out of the queue. Trudging down to the kiosk at the other end of the stand, two pies and two bovrils were ordered in misery before Jackie returned to his dad, who was starting to get anxious.

"What happened to you…did they accidentally find some meat in the pies and sent them off to the lab to be checked?"

Jackie took a sip of his meaty drink, paused and replied "just a queue dad, just a queue." His dad actually saying something funny for once and then Thistle turning on a first half display that was above and beyond the vast majority of expectations couldn't raise Jackie from his stupor and on the surface of it; the 0-0 half-time score line resonated with his feelings. Thistle had invested a hell of a lot of into that first half but hadn't made the breakthrough, James was upbeat, taking the positives but Jackie felt there was an ominous twist to come in the match.

He was right as with 8 minutes to go, a Thistle corner was swiftly cleared and one slip from the otherwise peerless left-back let the Kirkcaldy side through for a chance that wouldn't be squandered. Even with thirty yards between ball and goal, Jackie knew that the inevitable was coming and buried his head in his hands. The distant cheers from the away support and his dad's roar of "c'mon Thistle, we can still win this" were all the proof that Jackie needed to know that it was 1-0.

And so it finished, Thistle were still top of the table but their winning streak was over and sometimes, even the best teams just need a minor obstruction to send them into a downward spiral. The idea that fans behaviour can influence the outcome of a match is ludicrous, but it is no more ludicrous when you think about the other factors that influence a game of football. Confidence is often a significant factor in a game, the logic of knowing that you are a better player than your opponent is sometimes less powerful than actually believing this idea and so often, the lesser player comes away with victory in their individual battle. The Thistle team had shown itself to be the best in the league at this point but suddenly, the results stopped bearing this out. A 2-0 defeat from a game where the stats showed 72% possession, a 3-2 loss when the opposition only had four shots compared to Thistle's 17 and a 0-0 draw after Thistle hit the woodwork four times. If former Scotland boss Crag Brown was on hand, he would no doubt be dishing out the corner count and pointing out how stronger Thistle were in that area too but as well as being a former Scotland boss, he is also a former Clyde man, which makes his opinion not too valid at Firhill.

James McPherson was at a loss to figure out what had been happening. The way the games were panning out, it had to be luck that was the driving factor in the outcome of the match but he just couldn't place his finger on what had changed to make the season dip so dramatically. Over a family dinner, once the niceties of catching up had been dispensed with, James opened up to Jackie; "what is it son, it can't be us..we've done everything the same."

The home-made soup was still burning the back of his throat but Jackie felt the guilt of switching catering kiosks which was looking to be the fault of the poor run of form. That was preposterous; Jackie knew that, surely even his dad knew it but in light of all other things considered, it had to be it. Jackie was about to clear his throat and offer up his confession when James butted in, "I know what it is…that Terry down the road, I'm sure that Raith game he never went because his son had a birthday party. It's bloody his fault, wait until I see him down the pub next week. Sorry son…you were about to say?"

The silence was deafening, James hovering over the mashed potatoes staring at his son while Mrs McPherson busied herself in lining up the cutlery. "Oh…nothing dad, it's nothing, yeah, I think Terry did miss that game, maybe it was that." The rest of the dinner was spent discussing mundane non-football things with James starting to clock-watch to make sure he would catch the live game coming up shortly. Jackie decided to give the coffee a miss when a text saying some of the lads were out in town and were looking to make a night of it. "Anyone mind if I head off, a couple of things have come up?" asked James and even though he could tell that his mum would rather keep him around for longer, anything that saves her having to hear about football from James was welcome, there was no point in keeping the boy around if there's drink on the go. Boys will be boys…"bye mum…and I'll see you on Saturday dad, half two at the usual place?" Jackie was off and running before a response was given but with the air of superstition hanging heavy in the house, he knew the answer would be a yes.

Bunker on a Tuesday night, there's the sort of place you could set your watch by. Music that was far too loud, the temperature going through the roof, overworked bar staff, crowded dance floor and the impossibility of grabbing a seat unless you had popped in for lunch and decided to hang around. It was the perfect place for some midweek fun, and the rammed clientele were in agreement. After some squeezing, shifting and shaking, Jackie managed to meet up with the lads at the back of the venue where bottled beers were the order of the day. They were easier to carry from the bar but unfortunately, far easier to drink as well which meant that the rounds were flying thick and fast and the kitty money was being battered faster than a secondary school student who thinks he is brighter than his classmates. Inevitably, it was Jackie's turn to brave the crowds, and after attempting a Captain Scott "I might be gone sometime" speech, he fought his way to the bar and ordered up Corona's for all.

While at the bar, he thought he recognised a girl standing beside him but being unable to place a name to the face, he turned back to his drinks order. Just as he was about to walk away with 6 bottles, a tugging at his shirt grabbed his attention and the girl was talking to him. Jackie had absolutely no idea of what she was saying, such was the volume of the music but it was starting to dawn on him. Just at the point where the volume dipped to allow Jackie to hear "I know you from the football", he clicked that it was the kiosk lassie that had captured a piece of his heart. A gesture of hand signals, head pointing and a bizarre eyebrow movement got the point across that Jackie was going to drop the beers off with the boys but wanted a word with the girl...so they arranged to meet outside in the smoking section in five minutes.

Second guessing, Jackie took his coat out, in case he was out for a long time but it was really so he could play the chivalry card if needed, staying one step ahead was always the best way to find success.

Jackie arrived to find the girl outside, introducing himself with "hi, I'm Jackie, its Mary isn't it?" The girl gave him a quizzical look before bursting out laughing. "No, we all wear the name badges saying Mary...it's meant to be a joke, if anyone asks our name, we say Mary Hill." Tumbleweed rolled by at the thought of it and the two came to the conclusion that even though it was billed as a joke, it may well have been a tax dodge being employed by the club, which was obviously concerning. Not that there was any chance of EBTs being deployed in the Firhill kiosks, there the only use of EBT would be to ask for "Extra Bloody Tissues" after spilling the one warm cup of coffee down yourself

It turned out that Mary's real name was Stacey and the conversation was rattling back and forth between the two discussing where abouts in Glasgow they were from and where they like to go out, the important stuff. Stacey eventually asked the big question, "so where have you been in recent weeks, I haven't served you in a while." It was then that Jackie decided to come clean and the whole story unfolded, culminating in the rule about being unable to date fans of the club.

The same look that met the name Mary was delivered to Jackie, once again seeing Stacey dissolving in a fit of laughter. "That's not a rule silly; I just said that to get that idiot out of my face. If it was a rule, I'd probably be in trouble for hanging out about here wouldn't I...and you don't see me running off…and one thing you should know about me is that I like to play by the rules!"

It turns out that the rules involved Jackie getting the drinks in and handing his coat over to Stacey for a while, but these were rules that he could live by. The night was cut all too short by Stacey's pals wanting to move on and Stacey deciding to stay in the group. "Look, you know where I work, come see me on Saturday and we'll take it from there."

Off Stacey trotted to some other ridiculous late night establishment where the double measures were longer than most of the girl's skirts and Jackie returned to the boys, who would be staying where they were. After all, there was music, there was beer, there were girls and there was no need to come up against any other bouncers that night, especially not after how many beers had been consumed so far.

As hangovers went, it was one that Jackie could tolerate, and while the rest of the Thistle fan base was worried about the upcoming match against Falkirk, Jackie was positively bursting at the seams to get to Firhill on Saturday. Two-thirty pm Saturday eventually rolled around as Jackie met James and the footballing cycle kicked in again. A programme was bought, James scarf was still firmly in his pocket for now and the money was passed over for Jackie to get the pies in. Off he bounded as James wondered who was doing what that was affecting the outcome of the game. When matches are lost, it is easy to change your own routine but James was convinced that he was in the right and it was someone else in the wrong, which is why he stuck to his routine. All it needed was for things to fall back into line, for natural order to be resumed and Thistle would get back to winning ways.

Just at that point, Jackie reached the front of his more customary kiosk and was greeted with a beaming Stacey saying "Hello Sir, the usual is it?" "Yes please" responded Jackie and with service quicker than a manager reacting to a bad decision, his food and drink was served. "Excuse me sir, I think you'll need an extra napkin" and as Jackie took the additional items, he noticed there was a run of numbers on the top one, he nodded to Stacey, smiled and went back to his seat, thinking that all was well with the world again.

This was not being borne out on the pitch though, with the Thistle team having been seemingly replaced by folk who hadn't seen a football before let alone played the game. Thankfully their opponents were no brighter, playing as though they were coached by a baboon who was learning English one elongated syllable at a time. It is an over-used phrase but this generally was the sort of game that would get football stopped and even Jackie was thinking that his day was less than perfect; such was the hideous quality of football on show though.

The comments about things being darkest just before the dawn is not only an apt description of the morning skyline, it can sometimes sum up football games and teams too. Usually in the 89th minute when a match is being drawn, fans are straining forward to see the officials board go up, praying for there to be enough injury time to allow their team to grab a winner. On this occasion, the introduction of negative numbers would have been welcome but with two additional minutes to go, there was still a chance. Route 1 football isn't pretty but it can be effective and with a high humped ball from the Thistle goalkeeper spinning upwards on the first bounce, the Falkirk backline were mesmerised by the trajectory of the ball and perhaps the meaning of life. Whatever the reason, that one chance fell to the Thistle striker, he sclaffed at his shot but this was enough to deceive the Falkirk keeper and the ball trundled over the line.

As sexy football went, this was as attractive as spending a weekend with a rooster and a mongoose but as far as the Thistle fans were concerned, this was a party with the Victorias Secrets models! The scrappiest wins can sometimes get you going, and this knocked Thistle back into their stride just when it looked as though their season was collapsing in front of them. There would be bigger games to face and plenty of challenges throughout the season but as James McPherson turned to his son and uttered, "I told you son, I've still got this feeling that things are going to work out alright", the early evening sky got a bit lighter, and things seemed just fine.

With three points in the bag for the first time in weeks, the remnants of that pre-match pie still filling him up for the journey back into town and the number on the napkin nestled in his wallet, Jackie was of a mind to agree with his dad on this occasion, things were probably going to work out just fine.

Run Ron Run

It's glandular.

You're big boned.

You'll grow out of it.

There's just more of you to love.

It means you're happy with life.

These were just some of the lies that Ron would be told while growing up and would eventually tell himself to come to some sort of terms with his weight. He was big, not obese American TV cut a hole in the side of the house to get him out big…but he was big.

So big that he was called Fat Ron, and it wasn't a jokey nickname or an ironic term, it was a pretty factual state regarding Ronald and his appearance. It didn't make him a bad person, in fact, Ronald was quite a decent chap but of course, being that overweight meant that he would inevitably have periods of unhappiness. In amongst this would be fits of anger and then he would start to feel guilty about his anger, and he would return to eating. All of which meant that Ron was trapped in a colossal disappointment cycle, which was a bit ironic because he hadn't been near a bike in years…although it would be a reasonable starting place for him.

Enough was enough though; it was time for fat Ron to start reclaiming his body and after that, his life. So he walked. Not very far and not very fast but when he would previously take the car to the shops, he would walk. When he would have previously taken the bus into work, he would take the advice from TV adverts and get off one stop earlier. He also took to taking an additional shirt and deodorant into work with him so the sweat wouldn't be an issue.

The walking was difficult enough, but it was the food that was the killer for Ron. Cutting out the rolls in the morning, the bakery shop at lunchtime, the sweet treats late in the afternoon and then substituting the unhealthy dinner for something that at least came into contact with vegetables was a hard haul. However, he knew that it was all or nothing. Sure, there were a couple of bumps along the way. The odd empire biscuit here, the occasional pint and curry session there but slowly, Ron was making a difference.

The funny thing is, when you really need the kick up the backside, no one really wants to do it for you. However, when you start to get your life into order, people are falling over themselves to give you encouragement and praise. Perhaps you need to be able to show willing at first before other folk will dish out the praise but whatever it was; Ron noticed that other people were noticing him.

The girls on reception would stop him 3 to 4 times a week and ask for his weight loss tips. The canteen woman at work would jokingly complain that he was killing her pension fund by not stopping off in the afternoon anymore and his boss liked the difference. Every week Ron was feeling brighter, sharper and a bit more confident, which meant that his work was improving all the time. Half the folk in Glasgow need more confidence and half the folk need less confidence. There is probably the right amount of confidence overall in the city, it is just the balance with regards to certain people that is all wrong.

The imbalance was being maintained by the fact that while Ron was feeling all the better for the additional attention and praise being lavished upon him, it was starting to put a few people's noses out of joint. Ally Wallace was an associate of Ron's but certainly not a friend. The two spent very little time together and had very little in common. There was absolutely no need for Ally to have any input into what Ron was up to or to comment on Ron's performance at work. Of course, when has that scenario ever stopped anyone? Ally was, and is, a sleekit devious bastard. It was not enough for Ally to be doing alright, others had to suffer and struggle at the same time. The thought that someone else was getting praise angered Ally, and like a child, he would act out.

As usual, when guys get angry, you can usually trace the reason back to some girl, and half the time the girl doesn't even realise she was doing something wrong in the first place. Like so many people in the workplace, Ally had an unrequited love who he hoped would one day would notice him.

While Ally was sly and devious, he was also fairly average and unmemorable. Average height, average weight, average chat and his work was at a level not bad enough to cause him to be disciplined yet not good enough to earn him praise. He was your stereotypical number cruncher / pen pusher / water carrier that does the dirty work that keeps things ticking over. On some days, you'd doubt whether Ally's mum would be able to pick him out in a line-up let alone anyone else, so he had no chance of catching the eye of Tracey.

Tracey though, like everyone else, had commented on Ron's weight loss and praised him to keep going. Nothing more than that, nothing less than that, a nothing statement that we all sometimes make to pass the day or to give someone else a push. Even Ron never paid too much attention to it, he wasn't great with compliments so he decided to smile politely and say thanks as opposed to engaging with everyone. Tracey's comments could have come from anyone as far as Ron was concerned but this was not what Ally was thinking.

Ally was quickly devising a plan to show Ron up and put him back in his place. Sure he had lost weight but it is not as if he was slim yet, he was still at least 4 or 5 stone heavier than Ally was, so why should he be getting all of the praise. It was late on a Wednesday afternoon and Thursday morning saw the whole team receive an upbeat and "inspiring" lecture from their boss. Thursday was the new Friday and all that and the boss loved to think that he was pumping the team up with enough enthusiasm to freewheel into the weekend high on laughter and buzzing for the week. In reality, the team liked it because if they were listening to him, they weren't having to deal with clients or customers.

As people started filtering out to the lift or the stairs, Ally hung back, "I just want get a few things finished off" he said to no one in particular and before too long, the office was empty. Clearly the office was the same building and shell without people in it but it was quiet and a very different place to be. Even Ally didn't want to hang around for too long so once he waited to make sure that no one returned due to a forgotten umbrella or bag, he got to work.

He had a screwdriver in his desk, in fact he had a whole mini tool kit but it was the screwdriver he took out and headed straight to Ron's desk. On his knees, Ally quickly unscrewed some of the bolts that were keeping the chair in place. Worst case scenario, it falls apart over night and the first people in the office in the morning get to have a laugh at the fact that Ron's chair decided to commit suicide through the night as opposed to suffer another day of putting up with his considerable bulk. The best case scenario for Ally though was for the chair to hold in place until Ron went to sit on it and then it all collapsed under him, taking Ron down and turning some of that praise into tuts and criticism. The job done and the chair looking perfectly poised, Ally returned the screwdriver into his drawer and placed the two screws in there as well. Job done, now it was time to wait and see what the morning brought.

Perhaps he was unable to sleep at the thought of his genius or perhaps he was just a snidey bastard but Ally was in sharp the next morning. His mind was anything but focused on his job and he kept looking up to see if Ron was in or lumbering into the office. The chair was still in place, Ally had a slight panic when he thought about the cleaner perhaps knocking the chair off but that never arose.

At just before 9, the boss was loitering about, getting ready to give his grandiose energising speech of the week. It was at this point that Ally started to get concerned over the fact that Ron hadn't turned up yet. This would ruin everything thought Ally. Wouldn't it be like that big selfish fat bas…and just at that point, Ron came bounding through the door.

"Hey Ron, looking fab" said the boss as he then proceeded to make a clicking gun motion at Ron, which no doubt was meant to look trendy but looked as embarrassing as a father engaging with his eight year old son and their pals. Ron smiled politely, placed his jacket on the hook, placed his bag beside his desk, went to take his seat and crash.

Just as Ally had planned, the seat, without the screws, couldn't take Ron's weight, bringing him down to the floor. Immediately people turned to see what the commotion and a few people ran over to see if he was alright. Ron didn't feel hurt, at least not on the outside. It wasn't a big enough fall to cause any damage but the odd stifled laughter around the home was what hurt the most.

In reality, there were about four or five times the amount of people in the room showing genuine concern about Ron's well-being than were finding humour in the incident but that's never what you hear or focus on. To Ron, while he was nodding when people were asking if he was okay, all he could hear was the laughter ringing in his ears. Why here? Why now? Why not weeks or months ago when I was heavier than what I was.

The boss, standing up front and having no attention focused on him, rattled his keys off the projector, creating a jarring sound that stopped everyone in their tracks. Ron was back on his feet, the chair was in pieces, Ally was stifling laughter and the boss said, "Take five people…grab a coffee" and as he made his way back to his office, he asked Ron to follow him in.

If Ron thought the fall to the floor and the laughter was embarrassing, he had no idea how embarrassing things were going to get.

The boss, perched on his desk, "Now Ron, I like you and you've been doing great with your weight loss of late but this is a concern. A big concern. I can't have you putting yourself at risk every time you want to sit down." The absurdity of it all struck Ron as he now sank further into this seat than he had ever done before. "I'd like to arrange a meeting with HR next week Ron, lets talk some things over about health and safety. Hey, with the way this country is going, we'll probably have a few more big guys and girls like you working in the office, lets make sure that we are fully equipped to meet your needs."

Ron wanted the floor to open up and swallow him. None of this made any sense, five minutes ago he had arrived at work, sweaty and confident, got himself cleaned up for another productive day and then this. It seemed like he was back at square one, in fact, it seemed like he was back further than where he started.

At least back then when Ron started out in his fitness drive, no one noticed him, he could go about his day under the radar. Now though, everyone knew him recognised him and he would no longer be "Ron: The big guy who is working hard to lose weight", he would be "Ron: The big guy that broke his chair". What was the bloody point? Ron felt himself start to well up, weeks and months of hard work and suddenly it felt as though it was all for nothing. His boss, perhaps noticing that Ron was not reacting positively to what he thought was positive news broke the silence and said, "Tell you what Ron, you head off outside for a bit, get some fresh air, stretch your legs and make sure you are not stiff or sore."

Ron thanked his boss and made his way to grab his coat. As he did, Ally was standing in the passageway and instantly, he could see that Ron was close to tears. Most normal people would feel guilty for their actions but for Ally, this was the chance to finish Ron off.

"Stop blubbing blubber boy, you may slip on your tears of grease." With this, Ron shoved his coat on and headed for the door. "That's it….run Ron run…as fast as you can". Again, the laughter was ringing in Ron's ears as he made his way to the lift, the first time he had taken the lift in weeks. He was on autopilot, the muscle memory he had worked hard to ignore or diminish in recent weeks kicking back in, taking him to the place where he knew he wouldn't be laughed at.

"Hello stranger, no seen you in a while, what you after?" asked the till girl. Ron took a deep breath and then let out a sigh before saying, "Fuck it, two pies please love." The girl was a bit startled by the choice language coming from Ron but to be fair, if that was the only time she'd hear expletives in the store that morning, she'd be a happy girl. "There's a slight heat in them, is that okay?" Ron nodded as he settled the bill and made his way back out on the street.

Ronald was already feeling sickened by himself before he had even put one of those greasy pies to his lips but this was who he was. He had tried but when you get other people being dickish about life, what's the point in trying to work against the grain? Ron wasn't that happy when he was heavy and doing nothing about but he was certainly a lot unhappier when he was trying to do something about.

Nah, "it's time to get comfortable with you who are Ronald" thought Ron as he scrunched one of the pies up to the top of the bag and prepared to take a bite.

A smell that had been absent in life for so long filled his nostrils and Ronald took a second to breathe it in before he chomped down on the greasy treat.

"Ronald…what are you doing?" schreeched at him before he could hammer his molars down on to the savoury snack and as Ronald looked around, he saw old Mrs Johnstone standing behind him, looking rather cross.

"Just what is the meaning of this young man? I've seen you out walking every day and your mum has been telling me of how hard you have been sticking to your diet, what is this?"

Mrs Johnstone had the manner and demeanour of a primary school teacher and Ronald immediately felt as small as he was back in Primary 3, which was big for his age but considerably smaller than he was now. Without looking up, Ronald pushed the pie back down in the centre of the bag and went to utter some excuse or explanation but of course, he had none.

"I'm waiting young man…" said Mrs Johnstone and Ron told the story in full detail. It was painful to recall but the chat with the boss and the final stinging insult from Ally was the most hurtful thing. Mrs Johnstone reached out to Ron, took him by the hand and deftly swiped the bag out of his hand.

"That's the thing Ronald, some people are just not very nice, you can't let yourself be bullied or cowed down to by them." Mrs Johnstone rooted around in her bag, pulled out an apple and a cereal bar. "Now Ron, I'm not saying these are as tasty as those pies and I'm not saying that the cereal bar is too healthy either but they're better for you. I'll take one pie and put the other in the bin….and you get back into work with your head held high. Your mum's very proud of what you've achieved so far Ronald, keep it up."

That was exactly what Ron needed to hear, and he thanked Mrs Johnstone for her kind words. Such a polite boy thought Mrs Johnstone and Ron made his way back into the building and up the stairs. Entering back into the office, Ron noticed that there was a lot of commotion around his general work area. "Be strong Ronnie, be strong" he thought to himself. No doubt someone will have done something hilarious like draw a hole in the floor or set up some form of accident area. Brilliant, this isn't going to blow over too quickly he thought.

However, when he got closer, he saw that people were looking at the chair in close detail. "Hey Ron, did you know some of the screws were missing from your chair?" Ron looked on in disbelief as he poked his finger through the holes where the security of the chair was supposed to be maintained.

"Blooming hell big man, never mind you, wee Shona from accounts sitting on this chair would have brought it down" and there was laughter but not at Ron, this was a laughter that Ron could join in with. Shona laughed, Ron chuckled, and even the boss came out to grab a quick word with Ron, "Ignore that thing about HR Ron, lets' just put this down to a one-off."

There was a lighter and brighter mood in the office, almost as light as Ron was feeling. It was a strange thing though, what had happened to the screws. A few people took a look at the floor around Ron's desk but there was nothing in the way of the missing screws. A replacement chair was brought over, Ron gingerly sat on it, and when there was no reaction or problem, everyone carried about their day as usual.

Just before lunchtime, the boss announced "Look, it's been a crazy day, after work, let's get some beers and pizza in. Tracey will come round to take numbers of who is up for it and we'll get something arranged." It was the feel good day of the year in the office but Ron already decided that he'll be sticking to diet soft drinks and avoiding the pizza. He has chicken salad for tea tonight when he gets home but he can stay around for a while. The positive air was infectious and by the time Tracey got around to Ally's desk, he decided that it was time to make a move. Emboldened by the success of the Ron chair prank, Ally decided that it was time to give Tracey some good chat.

As she asked, "are you hanging around after work tonight?", Ally responded, "Oh aye and hey, as well as the beer, I have something that will help to liven up the party." Ally then went to open up his desk drawer to show off a few miniature bottles of vodka that he had in there but as he did, there was only thing that caught Tracey's eye.

"Hold on…why do you have screws in your desk?"

At that moment, it was akin to a stranger walking into a country and western bar. The chatter and buzz of the room stopped and everyone stopped and turned to look at Ally. Now it was Ally's turn to sweat as Tracey picked up the two screws and then passed them over to one of the maintenance staff. Within a minute, they had been placed back into Ron's original chair, and Ally had an awful lot of explaining to do.

Ron was puzzled, he didn't even really know who Ally was apart from that nasty jibe this morning, but that was after the chair incident. The party after work was a massive success with Ron helping himself to a diet coke and some side salad. Ally had already been escorted out of the building, guaranteeing that he would lose pounds in a manner that not even Ron could contend with.

All Jo Morrow's Panties

Jo Morrow was your stereotypical girl next door. She was pretty, confident, intelligent, polite and could hold her own when it came to the "banter". Life hadn't always been easy growing up in Castlemilk but with her mum and her dad's encouragement, things were going pretty well for the girl. She was in her Second Year at Strathclyde University and was on track to get great grades. Third and fourth year were going to be bigger challenges but at this moment in time, things were going pretty well.

For Dave McCluskey, Jo was the actual girl next door. For as long as Dave could remember, Jo and her family had been his neighbours and it seemed as though they were destined to grow up and date. They finally started dating near the end of 6th year of school after they realised it made too much sense to do anything else. Nearly two years down the line and things were going fairly well for the couple. Of course there had been ups and downs but in the grand scheme of things, there wasn't too much to complain about.

In fact, for Jo, there was just one problem in her life. It wasn't Uni, it wasn't money, it wasn't her friends and it wasn't boys. It was the fact that Jo was regularly having her underwear pinched from the washing line. No doubt there is a market for twenty year old girls' underwear but when it is being stolen from your washing line under cover of darkness, it can leave you feeling a little unsure of yourself. Jo tried to put it behind her but with every new theft, it ate away at her a bit more. After all, if it was just the knickers then it's not ideal but you can just about deal with it but you don't know what else might happen.

There are a lot of weirdos and nutters out there thought Jo, it was the south side of Glasgow we're talking about and Jo wasn't too fond of having to walk down the road by herself late at night. That aside, life was going swimmingly but sometimes you just need one thing to knock you off your stride.

Jo was walking home from the local shops one night when she spotted Lizzie Johnston. Those exposed roots can be spotted from 100 yards away and when Jo saw them, it was usually time to get her own head down. Pulling her hood over her head, Jo started to power walk, hoping it would be enough to avoid confrontation or a showdown. Almost there she thought, almost there.

"Hey Jo, how are you?"

Shit! Jo stopped, pushed her hood back down and waited to see what Lizzie had to say for herself. The perma-tanned boot never had a good to say about anyone so Jo was bracing herself for something cutting or biting. The rest of Lizzie's family were ok, Jo's mum was pally with Lizzie's mum but Lizzie was a nasty piece of work.

"My maw says you've been getting your knickers stolen."

Here it comes thought Jo, no doubt a slaggy or slutty comment is on its way.

"My Terry was telling me that your Dave was showing off a pair of your knickers to the boys."

The self-contented smile on Lizzie's face indicated that she was taking a hell of a lot of pleasure from this statement. Lizzie continued, "It's just…I would hate for my Terry to do something like that so I thought you would like to know."

Jo thought she could detect a sneer in Lizzie's voice but she thanked her, pulled her hood back up and made her way home.

Jo battered the front door, clumped up every stair and slammed her bedroom door so hard that people in the city centre were complaining about the sudden breeze. Jo knew that Lizzie was a cow that loved to cause trouble at but at that point in time, it all seemed to make sense.

It wasn't even the fact that Jo was raging about her underwear going missing anymore; she was more annoyed and angry about Dave going behind her back. Jo was so angry that she started to cry and she never noticed her mum had entered the room.

Good old mum, no matter the situation, she thought a hot tea and a Caramel Wafer was the answer to everything. Give her a suitcase packed with the very best from Tetleys and Tunnocks and she'd sort out that unpleasantness between Israel and Palestine before Emmerdale was due to start.

So Jo unloaded and mum listened.

"I trusted him mum" said Jo but as Jo's mum patted her hand, Jo knew she wasn't going to like the next response.

Mum said, "So you're taking the word of that wee stirrer Lizzie Johnston? Her maw's a gossipy besom but Lizzie is something else entirely. You calm yourself down love and have a wee chat with Dave later on."

Mum left the room; Jo finished her tea and closed her eyes. Whether the crying had taken a lot out of Jo or mum had slipped something into her tea who knows but she was very quickly out for the count.

The tapping at her door and then her dad bellowing "There's your tea love" brought Jo out of her slumber and she was feeling slightly punch drunk as she made her way downstairs. Jo stopped at the door, took a deep breath and composed herself. She walked into the room, pulled out her chair and as she was in the process of sitting down, her little brother started to laugh.

"Haha, it's Krusty!" Jo froze as he continued, "Hey Hey kids"

Jo's mum snapped "Stop acting the clown Mark" but this unfortunate choice of words only heightened Mark's reaction. "How come I can't act like a clown yet Lizzie gets to look like one" and everyone bar Lizzie burst out laughing.

Lizzie hadn't checked her makeup after waking up but a quick look in the dining room mirror indicated exactly why the joke was on her. Okay thought Lizzie, may as well roll with it as opposed to fighting against it! "Tears of a clown" joked Lizzie, "although to be honest Mark, it is more of a panda look than a clown."

You can always rely on your family to take the mick out of you and put you back on the right track. Dad ran through all of his circus jokes while mum laughed and smiled politely. When dinner was over, mum said, "You young lady, sort your makeup out and speak to Dave. You my boy, you can do the dishes for all of your clowning round."

"Aww mum" said Mark as Jo stuck her tongue at him and started to hum the circus theme tune.

Okay Jo, compose yourself she thought. She scraped the tear sodden make up from her face, applied a new layer and took another deep breath.

Dave may have only stayed next door but with modern technology, there was no need to leave the room. Jo fired up the laptop, jumped on Skype and sent Dave a message. A few seconds later, he responded and the pair were chatting by video as though they were sat together in the same room.

The usual chit chat and lovey-dovey meanderings rounded out the conversation before Jo thought it was best to get it over and done with.

"So get this, that cow Lizzie Johnston says you've been the one stealing my underwear."

"She's mental Jo, a poisonous boot" said Dave.

Jo replied, "I know that, she said you had shown the boys a pair of my pants."

Even allowing for the slight delay in online communication, there was an uncomfortable pause. Jo wondered if the screen had frozen before Dave said, "Yeah about that...I can explain."

The bastard. "You can just fuck off" said Jo as she shut down the connection and slammed her laptop shut. Within seconds her mobile phone started to ring which Jo duly ignored. The utter creep, Dave had obviously taken her underwear, the dirty pervert. That's us finished thought Jo as once again, the waterworks started.

Over the next few days, Dave made numerous attempts to contact Jo but she ignored them all.

It had been a long and rough week for Jo. She was able to keep her head down at Uni but she was struggling to find the motivation for anything else, including her tutoring role. Jo could normally do maths in her sleep but she was struggling to keep herself and her pupil entertained.

"Are you ok?" the youngster asked.

"Yes, why?"

"It feels like you want to be here as much as me and I hate maths."

Jo smiled. "I've just got a lot to think about but c'mon, maths is fun. Yayyyyy."

"Booo" replied the kid, giving maths a big thumb down. That was enough to snap Jo out of her mood for the rest of the lesson but by the time she got home, she was back to being the upset girl of the past week. This is hardly a rare occurrence for any 20 year old girl, particularly one with such a conundrum to weigh up, but it wasn't like Jo. Jo's dad tried to cheer her up but you have to be in the right frame of mind to tolerate his jokes. They were for a select audience and all of his puns and wisecracks were best left in the 1970s. Not that they were blue or rude…they were just awful jokes!

So again, it was left to mum to sort her out. "Right my girl, Friday night, you, me and your auntie Pat are heading into town. Some drinks are very much in order so keep it free." Jo didn't even try to put up a fight, it had been a while since she had been out on the town with her mum and auntie Pat and it always ended up in some sort of commotion or story.

Much of the fun in going out on a Friday night was the getting ready element and with dad and Mark packed off to the cinema, the girls quickly finished off their dinner and started getting themselves glammed up for the evening. Auntie Pat had brought wine, vodka and shots and a fair dent was being made in them before they were halfway through doing their hair.

"It's always a cheap night out with your auntie Pat" said Jo's mum, and this was because you were always half canned before you even left the house. Eventually, the girls called a taxi and made their way into town. The Lloyds on West George Street was never going to be Jo's first choice for a Friday night out in town, but it was cheap, it had music on and there was a space to dance. It was all she needed to have a good evening out with her mum and aunt.

The Woo Woos kept on flowing and such was the good times, fuelled by affordable booze and naff yet danceable music, the night flew by. There were quite a few guys striding up to get the girls' attention but most of them were shooed away with the sound of raucous laughter. This was a girlie night out and it was going to take a lot more than a cheap shirt, cheaper aftershave and the promise of a cocktail pitcher to let a guy into their group that evening.

By the time midnight rolled around, Jo's mum was absolutely smashed and it was time to pour her into the taxi. She was sleeping and while auntie Pat was up for sending her home and continuing the night, Jo decided that she had better get her home. "Aye, you're a good lassie Jo…I'm going to meet some friends, here's money for the taxi and tell your mum I'll phone her tomorrow night."

Before the taxi had even reached Union Street, Jo had her mum slumped on her shoulder, snoring away. Brilliant thought Jo, dad is going to love this. The taxi driver tried to pass off some inane chat but Jo wasn't very receptive. The snoring from her mum made it hard for her to hear what he was saying and she generally phased out when taxi drivers talked at the best of times.

Eventually pulling up in front of Jo's house, the driver had the good grace to ask if Jo needed a hand but she responded with a polite, "I'm good thanks", as she handed over the money auntie Pat gave her. She may not have been great company for the driver but at least she was giving him a healthy tip.

"Right, up you get mum" said Jo, as she swung the door open and roused her mum onto her feet. For any neighbour looking out of their window, it would have been a fair old sight as Jo struggled to the front door balancing her mum along the way. It was not as if Jo was the definition of sobriety but as is usually the case, if one person is not as drunk as the other, they manage to look fresh faced and sprightly heeled in comparison. As Jo fidgeted the key into the lock, the door sprung open with dad saying, "I'll take this from here". Mum was bundled up the stair as Jo made her way into the kitchen for some juice and a raid of the breadbin.

Before too long, dad came back downstairs. "So princess, did you have a good night?" Jo had a mouthful of sandwich but the enthusiastic nodding of her head seemed to suggest that all was well with the world. "Good, glad you had fun, your mum will be paying for it in the morning. You know darling, if you ever need to talk, I'm here as well."

Jo took a massive gulp…finished off her sandwich and kissed her dad on the forehead. "Thanks dad, but I'm good, it's all good." She then made her way into the kitchen, put some rubbish in the bin and poured herself a glass of water. As she did, she looked out into the garden and noted that there was a full line of washing out, including her underwear.

"Night dad."

Jo made her way upstairs, put the glass of water beside her bed and went to close her curtains. As she did, she looked out and saw Dave stumble out of a taxi. It had been a week since Jo last spoke to him, one of the longest periods of time she had not spoken to Dave since she knew him. There had been a couple of family holidays on either side but away from that, this had definitely been the longest spell. She decided she would change that tomorrow and went to her bed.

The next morning, Jo awoke and went downstairs for breakfast. Dad was sitting there reading the papers. "Tea and toast Jo? I don't think your mum will be up anytime soon and Mark is away playing football."

Jo replied, "No you're fine dad, you read the paper, I'll get my own." Jo went to fill the kettle and looked outside. The washing line was still busy, bustling with the variety of clothes from the Morrow family, all apart from the gap at the left hand side. "You have to get be kidding me" exclaimed Jo as she made her way to the door and went outside. Looking around the ground and seeing that there was nothing on the ground or which had been misplaced, she came back inside, fuming.

"It's happened again dad. Someone has made off with my underwear." Jo was raging. Her knickers had still been on the line when she went to her bed in the early hours and yet they weren't there in the morning. She didn't want to say for definite but she knew that Dave was making his way home at this point. That sealed the deal for Jo and any thought that she had of a reconcilement was out of the window.

After some tea and toast, Jo made her way up to the room and started grabbing all of the presents and nick-nacks that Dave had presented her with over the years. She placed them all into a box, sealed it up and left it on her bed. She showered, got changed, took the box next door and rang the doorbell. She thought of waiting but decided to leave. As Jo slammed her door shut, the front door of the McCluskey door opened to a box of surprises.

Jo went back to her bed, waiting for the phone call or chap at her door but it never came. Before too long, she fell asleep.

Eventually, Jo rose and made her way downstairs only to see her neighbour, from the other side of the house, sitting talking with dad.

"Oh hi Mr Wallace" said Jo as her dad stood up. "You better sit down love; Mr Wallace has something to say."

This was never the start of a pleasant or positive conversation and Jo had a sinking feeling in her stomach. The worst thing is, she didn't have a clue as to what was going on.

"I'm really sorry to say this Jo, but well, your items that have been going missing, it was our dog."

Given that Jo had lived in Castlemilk all of her days, she had heard some tall tales in her time but this was a whole different level. "What?"

I went into Towser's dog house to give it a brush out and in the corner was a bunch of your underwear. I'm really sorry, it seems as though he was the one that had been stealing from you.

This was absolutely ludicrous thought Jo, how on earth did that wee dog manage to get into her garden and then steal her underwear. "I'm sorry Mr Wallace, this just sounds bizarre, I don't see how this happened" said Jo as they all took a walk outside into the garden.

It turns out that one of the fencing slats between the two gardens was loose and Towser was able to fit through quite comfortably. From here, he was able to bound on to the big ceramic pot, onto the bird table and from there he could leap over to the clothes rope closest to the wall. The side of the wall where Jo's mum always hung Jo's clothes because she didn't want her daughter's clothes out in the middle of the garden.

Just as this point, Towser came scampering through the gap in the fence, took one look up at the three of them standing there and then promptly bolted back through the fence.

"I really am very sorry dear, I'll have that fence nailed up later today and please take this money to get some replacements for your…" Mr Wallace stuttered off, he wasn't overtly comfortable talking to his young neighbour who he had known for many years about her underwear. Jo sensed this, graciously accepted the money and said, "Let's say no more about it."

Later on that day, over a cup of tea, Jo's mum, still feeling a bit fragile and slightly behind the times, said, "Hold on dear, if the dog from next door was stealing your underwear, that means it wasn't Dave."

Mark piped in, "No mum, Dave's mum and dad talk about the dog next door…and they mean Jo." That earned Dave a skelp around the ear but he thought it was worth it. Jo returned to her mum, "I don't know mum, he still admitted that he was showing the boys my underwear, so maybe he took a pair from me as well."

"He didn't really admit that though did he love? You never gave him the chance to explain, maybe you should later on."

Later that evening, Jo was popping down to the shops when she saw Dave coming up the road. In the past few weeks, this would have been her cue to take evasive action but she decided to confront him. Jo explained the story of how Mr Wallace came over and that it was Towser who had been stealing from her. "So what was the story about you showing boys my underwear?"

Dave stuttered, hummed and hawed before explaining it was a stupid dare but he couldn't go through with stealing Jo's underwear. Instead, the first time he was coming through town, he stopped into Primark and in addition to buying a lot of rubbish for himself that he didn't really need, he picked up a pack of female underwear.

"It wasn't fun going through that till let me tell you Jo" as he pulled out a receipt from his wallet. When you hung up on me that day, I dug out my receipt and I've been wanting to show you ever since.

Jo was still really annoyed. Dave had still showed a pair of underwear to the boys and intimidated that they were hers. That was still a complete no no as far as Jo was concerned. There was also the fact that Dave thought it was acceptable to suggest that Jo bought her knickers from Primark. Jo had been insulted a fair bit in her life but that was certainly a slap in the face she was not impressed with.

However, it seems as though the worst of her fears weren't true and she felt herself warming to the fact that Dave had at least kept hanging on in there.

The two of them stood in the light evening breeze for what seemed like minutes before Dave piped up, "So…can we go out for a drink or a meal at some point and see what we still have?" Jo smiled, paused and said, "Maybe, I've got a date with Towser this week and I'd like to see how that pans out." Dave stared at the girl before she burst out laughing, drawing the same response from him. The two of them hugged for the first time in weeks and started heading towards the shops together.

Heroes Inn

"Bloody do-gooders. Convincing people to give up the fags may seem like a good idea for the Health bodies and the Government but I'm telling you Jamesie, it's utter crap for the rest of us."

The day ended in a Y so it was tradition that Jamesie would have to listen to Danny rant and rave about something. Most guys would head to the pub and detail their problems to a sympathetic barman or barmaid but it seems as though Jamesie had it all the wrong way round. Once again he found himself on the end of another one of bar owner Danny Cairneys's relentless complaints about what was wrong with the world and how this meant bad news for Danny.

"Sure, they may be saving people's lives but that just means that we've got more years to live in this hell-hole, and it's the worst years you get extended, never the good ones."

Jamesie initially thought that this was an altruistic thought from Danny, no doubt looking out for his fellow man with the compassion and empathy of a Saint. It then dawned on him that if this was the case it would be the first time ever for Danny and that there must have been an ulterior motive.

Jamesie broke his silence saying, "You're not wrong Danny and I bet your takings have been hurt since this smoking ban."

They had indeed and it would be fair to say that the pub had seen better days. The smoking ban was just one factor that was harming the pub that had been in Danny's family for three generations. Smokers weren't coming along anymore because they resented having to huddle outside in the cold, wind and the rain to get their nicotine fix. Of course, those conditions were the external elements for summer, in the winter there was snow to worry about and the winds upgraded to a gale.

If that was the only thing that the pub had to contend with, they may just get away with it but there was a lot more trouble in store for a public house in Glasgow. The supermarkets were slaughtering bars and pubs thanks to cheap booze. Why come to the pub and pay over the odds for moderate lager and average company when you can be just as miserable at home for much less money?

With Sky hammering the prices up to show the fitba and punters able to watch virtually every game going on a dodgy stream at home, the licensed trade was getting battered from every angle and there didn't seem to be any way to give punters an excuse to come along.

"We've tried it all mate and nothing works" said Danny and the shortfall in takings certainly wasn't due to a lack of effort on the pub's behalf. There was a bingo night but Danny quickly found that bingo players weren't drinkers. In fact, he had to chip out three to five players every night for sneaking their own drinks in with them. Danny had dealt with the great and the good, the bad and the scum from the local area but he had never witnessed such venom, anger and stubbornness as when he was trying to tell bingo players that they were being prevented from playing the rest of the game. He was close to calling the polis one night but he knew the consequences of that would have been long-term and fairly damaging for the pub.

They tried to run a movie night but most folk had already seen the films that Danny was lining up to show. He did manage to get a dodgy copy of one of the latest films in the cinema but that turned out to be a disaster. The first five minutes were going brilliantly and then the guy in the row in front of the person operating the camera in the cinema shifted his position and blocked the screen. It was funny for a couple of seconds but when the pub attendees realised that this would be their view for the next 80 minutes, they were quick to demand a refund. It actually cost Danny money that night. "Here Danny, what about a karaoke night?" asked Jamesie.

"Tried that mate, did not end well."

Again, Danny was the master of the understatement in his explanation. It turns out that Kelly Jessop doesn't like anyone else getting to sing 'Bad Romance' by Lady Gaga before she does. Danny would have been quite happy for both girls to sing their version over the course of the night but Kelly wasn't as fond of that idea. So she waited until Michelle Dawes took the stage to belt out the hit and then leapt up, grabbed the microphone and smashed her two front teeth in. The fact that they were falsers meant that the damage wasn't as bad as it could have been but it was more than enough to ensure that karaoke time was over in the pub.

"What about proper bands?" asked Jamesie and the shaking of the head from Danny said more than words ever could. This had been another attempt that had failed miserably and again, actually cost Danny money. He promised to give playing bands a bunch of beer (stuff that was close to its expiry date) and told them to bring all of their pals along. That was fine apart from the fact that people in local bands were the most unsociable people in the local area. Even the weird trainspotters have more of a collective gang mentality than this lot. That should have given the pub another opportunity to reel folk in but trainspotters aren't the biggest of boozers either.

So with the regular attendees staying away or at least supping up early after the first tuneless track from the local wannabes that are too cool for the X-Factor and none of the band's fanbase turning up, Danny was treated to a one man show. This isn't a bad evening out but when the one man is the actual barman watching the performance, it all gets a little bit pointless.

"Alright mate, here's one for you" started Jamesie and before Danny could tell him to shut up, there came an idea that was so simple that it could actually work.

"The thing about new bands is that even the good ones aren't going to come across well in this place. What you need is a band playing something that everyone knows, get a tribute band in…some of the tribute bands are huge."

This was an excellent idea and it was one that Danny agreed with. In recent years he had shelled out cash to see The Bandit Beatles and that Aussie Pink Floyd mob. There was that fake Abba mob raking it in and there was even that fat guy who looked a bit like Robbie Williams but couldn't sing playing at Hampden. Oh wait, no, that was Robbie Williams, still, the lassie love it and where the lassies go on a Friday or Saturday night, the boys will follow. "Jamesie, my boy, you're onto a winner."

For the first time in weeks, certainly the first time since the landlord down the road got lifted for selling moonshine vodka, Danny felt that there was something to be positive about it in the pub trade. Mind you, just when you felt that life was starting to roll your way, it has a habit of poking you in eye and then kicking you in the stomach when your defences were down.

The cost of hiring a local tribute act was way beyond the budget that James could stretch to. Admittedly his budget was along the lines of plenty of pints and two packets of crisps for every member but this was a million miles away from what was being asked for. It wouldn't have cost much more to book the real Rolling Stones for the pub compared to what these clowns were asking for! They didn't even look like the Stones although to be fair, if you're a big believer that Charlie is the main man in the Stones, this group were well acquainted with a touch of Charlie.

It was then that Danny struck upon the idea to end all ideas. He needed a covers band to play the big hits and keep the punters rolling in and then rolling out pished out at the end of the night. Some of the local bands he had hired previously were in dire need of an audience and to be honest, some tunes that people would like. It was a match made in Heaven thought Danny and he was quickly on the phone to one of the acts.

"Hello Joe, it's Danny fae the pub here."

"Aye mate, I don't know who stole that crate of beer, that could have been anyone" was the quick reply. Danny thought to himself you little bassa but continued, "Naw, shut up son, I've got a proposition for you, one that will help your band, pop into the pub the morra and I'll tell you all about it."

Joe rolled in about 4pm, a quiet time in the day, but not so different from the busy times of the day. Danny outlined what he was looking for. He wanted Joe and the band to play every Friday and Saturday night, blasting out covers of some of the biggest bands in the music industry. Danny would sort out the wigs and costumes as long as the band learned the songs. It was a deal that suited everybody so Joe and Danny quickly started to plan the most important things, what bands would they play tribute to.

Given the sort of clientele that Danny was dealing with, there was no point in being too contemporary. It is not as if Joe's band were going to transform into One Direction or Little Mix overnight but that wasn't going to bring in the punters even if they could. From the 60s to the 90s was what the pub was looking for and the more hits and choruses the better.

"Right, I think The Eagles will go down well with our crowd, learn them some of their songs, now what name can we use for them?" asked Danny, who was astounded by the response.

"How about The Birds?" said Joe and Danny paused, looking for a laugh, a smirk or some sort of reaction that would indicate that Joe was at least in on the joke.

Nothing.

"You know that there was a really popular band called The Byrds?"

"Haha, the birds…I bet they got a lot of laughs…when they were running late did anyone ever ask where's the birds? Magic."

Joe was as stupid as he was glaikit looking but at least he could play the guitar a bit. Danny realised that he would need to go more mainstream at first and within minutes, the line-up was starting to take shape. The Friday night would see the group perform as Oasis and on the Saturday, they would play as The Beatles. Danny was preparing himself for the fact that some wag would quip about the same band playing two nights in a row but as long as the punters came along and spent their cash, he could take all the snidey remarks and failed comedy routines that were thrown at him.
The Stones, The Who, U2 and Blur were all added to the list, which would surely be more than enough to get these nights up and running.

Joe headed off to inform the band of the money and regular gigs that were coming their way and Danny set himself the most important task, coming up with the fake tribute band names. This would be one of the most important tasks. The right name, capturing humour while making sure people know what was in store, would be crucial in building a crowd.

Taking Non Jovi and Peat Loaf as the benchmarks, Danny poured himself a whisky and tried to get creative.

Nawasis

Blurry

The Who Are You Talking Tae?

Haw, You Two

The Beat Its

The Strolling Moans

Some were better than others, but they would do the job. Danny started firing up the posters around the pub and the news started to spread. The local punters wouldn't have bothered their backsides coming in for a new band or one that they hadn't heard of but give them the sniff of celebrity and they fall over themselves.

And so it came to Friday night and a full hour before the band was due to come on, the pub was full. Danny had called in all the bar staff and even then they were struggling to keep up with the demand for lager or vodka. Even more worryingly, they couldn't keep up with the demand for pint tumblers. This was great news but it meant hurrying folk up and sending staff out to collect as many tumblers as possible. This was taking folk away from the bar but on the whole, the atmosphere was electric. If you think about all the problems a bar can have, not having enough pint tumblers to go round is one that a bar manager can put up with.

Backstage…well, in the store room, the band was psyching themselves up and they could hear the buzz of noise and anticipation that was building up on the other side of the room. The sound check had gone alright earlier on in the day and it is not as if they had to stretch their clothing budget to wear clothes that were passable for Oasis. The line of black masking tape on their foreheads to replicate the Gallagher monobrow was perhaps a comedic touch too far, but Joe felt it would help the band come across well to the audience.

He needn't have bothered.

It was going to take a lot more than a badly applied piece of masking tape to a couple of foreheads to win this crowd over. Up stepped Tony, in his best Liam swagger, to the microphone and before he could utter a word, whizzzz, a bottle of Becks flew past his ear and exploded on the wall behind the drum kit. Tony was shaken, the colour draining from his face as Joe stepped bolshily forward. Perhaps it was the pre-gig Jager flowing through him or maybe he believed he was channelling the youthful spirit of Noel Gallagher but his response of "alright dickheads, you fancy some of this do you?" only resulted in more bottles being thrown towards the stage.

In one way, Danny was horrified, this was a terrible way to treat any young band and he would need to ensure that he got the bottles and glass cleaned up. In another sense though, this was wonderful news. If it created a bit of a story, it would keep folk coming back and if people wanted to drink half a bottle, chuck it and then come and buy another bottle, he could see that being a money winner.
Still though, better step in here he thought.

Danny moved round the bar, jumped on stage and shoved Joe behind him. "Awright simmer down, simmer down." Looking around the room, Danny was gripped by a slight sense of panic, this was perhaps not his best idea, he needed to get off this stage quickly. "We've got a great band with all the hits here, let them put some sunshiiinnnnneee into your miserable lives."

The Liam Gallagher style sneer that had been nicked from Johnny Rotten elicited a cheer and Danny knew that he was on a roll. "Look, give these lads a chance and they'll give you a good night. I don't care what some might say (cheer from the crowd), none of you lot are going to live forever (even louder cheer), so shut up, behave yourself and we'll all have a good night....or you know, whatever"

The last pun got a great response and Danny mouthed "start playing now" as he jumped off stage. He loved the limelight but he had given up on Oasis after the second album so he didn't really have many more titles in mind that he could have milked but it seemed to do the job.

The opener of 'Rock N Roll Star' immediately took the edge off of the crowd and by the time 'Wonderwall' was rolled out, the lighters were in the air and the audience was swaying more than old Captain Jones at the bar. His problem was purely medical, or so he said, but with the other lot, they were caught up in the moment of a good night out.

The rest of the set meandered its way to the end without any hitch, although the crowd singing during 'Don't Look Back In Anger' would have been enough to have the gig stopped on humanitarian purposed. Bloody hell thought Danny, I'm just lucky karaoke night got ditched when it did!

The band shuffled off stage, back into the cupboard and the applause continued. It evolved into the "one more tune" chant with the stamping of the floor and the clapping of hands setting up a rhythm that the act couldn't ignore.

Back on they shuffled and in lieu of any other tunes, they played 'Wonderwall' and 'Don't Look Back In Anger' again. The crowd went mad...but in a good way. The power of drink isn't that strong that the crowd had forgotten that these songs had already been played, it was just the fact that these songs were clearly the favourites. Why mess about playing anything else? It was a reminder to Danny and it was an early pointer to the band that keeping things simple and giving people what they want is the secret to success.

The band was eventually allowed to finish for the night and the bar was celebrating its most successful day in years. Takings were up by a huge amount and people were asking what time the gig the following day started. Danny thought that he'd have to start selling tickets for the gigs if this demand was going to keep up.

At the end of the night, with the doors locked and the broken glass and spilled beer swept away into the bin and the memory books, Danny was enjoying a quiet after hours lock in with Jamesie. Jamesie was sitting with a smug look on his face. At first, it looked as though his tribute band idea was going to result in the band getting killed and seeing Jamesie receive a well-aimed toe up the backside from Danny but in the end, it was a roaring success.

"That was mental Danny, by the end you would swear that the punters thought it was Oasis, have you been selling dodgy beer again?" The two laughed, probably knowing that was closer to the truth at times than anyone would care to admit but Danny pulled himself together.

"Nah mate, it was just about getting them to believe in it. They know it wasn't Oasis but let's face it, when you've got nothing else; all you need is something to keep you going. All they folks that were in the night. If they were lucky enough to have jobs, their jobs are shite and coming in here was the first thing they've looked to forward to all week. The ones without jobs, Christ, they've had it even tougher."Jamesie nodded but he knew Danny was off on one.

"They all know it's a tribute act, they're not that daft, but they're not going to say it are they? They're not going to be the one saying to their pal or their wife to calm it doon because it's no the real thing. No one is going to break ranks and admit it. This is as close to the real thing as they can get these days, so they grab it and I'm going to do my best to help them grab it, because you know something, it's the only thing that some of the poor gits have got in their life."

Jamesie was thinking that Danny wasn't a bad guy. He was right; it had been a rough old time of late for loads of folk in the local community. If putting on a tribute act was enough to put a smile on folk's faces, why shouldn't Danny give people what they want? If a few more folk did their bit for the community, it would be a lot nicer place to stay. Aye Jamesie was thinking that Danny wasn't that bad a fellow when Danny broke the silence, "Anyways, if being sold a tribute act is enough to make these mugs happy, I'm more than happy to take their money off them. If I don't, someone else will, because mugs and their money are always parted Jamesie, always parted."

That was more like the Danny Jamesie knew and tolerated.

George Square She Goes Again

"Merry Christmas Tony…have a decent one, see you in the New Year" were the last words Tony heard before leaving the office and heading up Bath Street. Christmas Eve morning in work was a joke and with the office shutting at midday, it was hardly worth the effort of turning up. Still, turning up and taking advantage of the early get away at least legitimised heading to the pub at such a sprightly hour. Regardless of the festive season, the weather in Glasgow was as damp and grey as you would expect for mid-December. This is not the Christmas Eve that they show in films or TV shows, and as Tony headed for the nearest pub, he was hoping to put all thoughts of Christmas out of his mind.

Just as he was crossing the road, one of his colleagues came up behind him and pushed and pulled Tony to and from the road. "Saved your life there Tony mate…you owe me one. We're all going to George Square for a skate and a laugh, do you fancy it?"

"I really don't mate, I'm just planning on getting blitzed and falling asleep in front of the telly and then waking up tomorrow with a raging hangover. Skating is not part of that plan."

"Don't give us your bah humbug talk big man, c'mon..there's a few of us heading down, come down for one skate and then you can drink yourself into oblivion."

Sensing he was not going to get peace until he relented, Tony decided it was best to get it over and done with. It wasn't that he disliked his colleagues, he just wanted peace and quiet. It had been a rough year and celebrating Christmas was not high on Tony's agenda.

The walk down to the Square was full on excited chatter about the festive period, and where and when they were spending it. Tony remained quiet, but Stacey, the admin girl was happy to talk for everyone. "My Kevin is taking me out tonight for dinner and then tomorrow we're going to his mum and dads for lunch before my mum and stepdad cook dinner in my new kitchen. Its bigger than their house so it makes sense, I said I'm not cooking though…can you imagine, the turkey will be bigger than me…no, I've gave my maw a set of keys, and when we're visiting Kevin's family, she'll be over at mine getting the dinner ready."

The buzz around the town was palpable with Buchanan Street looking an ungodly mess. Panic had set in for a great number of people, not all men as the stereotype would suggest but every manner of Glaswegian. Tony thought it was great to see that Christmas was the great leveller, making fools out of all social backgrounds, but he couldn't help but feel a twinge of jealousy towards the group of guys who were clearly heading to Waxy's.

"Err, how about we stop in for a quick one before we hit the ice….give us a bit of confidence" asked Tony, the first time he had spoken since walking with the group.

"Naw, you're just fine there Tony, I'll be on my arse enough on the ice rink without a drink, skating first and then you get a drink, that was the plan" chirped in Jenny, a girl that used to sit across from Tony but had moved to a different department. Tony didn't think he knew everyone in the group, but there were enough faces he was on nodding terms with to just about make it bearable. One skate they say…that's all it will take to get it over and done with.

Even though George Square was the scene for some of the pivotal moments in Glasgow's history, it still held a certain kind of magic when it was tarted up to the high heavens. A lot of the majesty had been stripped from the Square over the years, but with the daylight fading, the twinkling of the Christmas lights and the big wheel could put a smile on anyone's face.

"Right everybody, c'mon…the sooner we get on, the sooner we get off" shouted James but was quickly shot back with "Is that what your missus says to you?" As the old saying went, this lot were "mad enough without a drink" which didn't actually mean they were mad…but it didn't necessarily translate into them being the life and soul of the party either.

Much to his dismay, having size 8 feet ensured there were plenty of skates in his size, and before he knew it, Tony was gingerly walking up the steps, onto the ice rink and boom, right on his arse! When there are 12 year olds skating by you shouting "she fall over, she fall over" it is hard to retain a sense of dignity and Tony was all for storming back off the ice. However, as he was getting to his feet, Pauline, a relatively new girl from the office, held out a hand to give some extra balance.

"Don't you listen to them Tony, just cause they wee jessies have been skating half their life on this rink doesn't mean you should be a natural. Hold on to me and we'll go round a few times, you'll see it's no so bad." Before Tony could react, Pauline had grabbed hold of his arm, and after taking a second to steady herself, she pushed off slowly. Tony just about managed to react in time, and even though he resembled a drunk penguin with his wobbling approach, he was off and running…or skating as the case may be.

Time seemed to slow down as the two of them made their way around the rink in a slow but steady fashion. It was certainly a different way to see the city, and it gave Tony time to look at the surroundings. Life in Glasgow can pass you by quite quickly, and it's not as if many locals spend a lot of time in George Square examining their surroundings. The square is commonly a cut-through to the station, to the

Merchant City, to Uni, to the shops or to Greggs, but when you are circling in a short radius looking around you, it is easy to see a bit more. Tony had plenty of reasons to be grumpy this Christmas and those that knew him weren't begrudging him taking some time for himself but you don't need to take yourself completely out of the game.

"Right big man, that's enough for me, fancy a coffee?" asked Pauline but Tony was in a world of his own as he glided across the rink. A dig to the ribs got his attention as Pauline put the brakes on, with Tony following suit. "You were lost in a wee world there Tony…you can carry on if you wish, but I'm going to grab a hot drink." "Aye, I'll come with you" replied Tony as he held on to the perimeter wall and made his way to the exit gap.

Just as Tony and Pauline were making their way off the rink, one of the goading youngsters went skating by and slipped of his own accord. Before Tony could react, Pauline was quickly laughing and pointing at the kid; "aye, no funny now is it?" but to be honest, the reaction from all around, including the 12 year olds mates was of genuine mirth and merriment. To his credit, the fallen youngster managed to retort with; "good to see your bird has got a better comeback than you ya bawbag" but when you're shouting this when lying on your back on an ice rink, it's never going to sound too cool.

After handing back their skates and entering the covered food and drink enclosure, Tony said "you grab some seats, and I'll get the drinks in. Coffee you said?" "Milky and one sugar please" was the response as Tony made his way to the overpriced beverage section. You can say what you want about Glasgow retailers, but they certainly know how to gouge their customers.

Upon sitting down and handing over the coffee, Tony had barely drawn breath before Pauline asked; "So are you alright

Tony. You always seem pretty quiet in work, and I noticed you didn't seem too keen to come here today?" At first Tony was hesitant but perhaps caught up in the spirit of the moment, and the season, he started opening up to a near stranger in a way that he hadn't done before.

The pair sat closely as Tony talked of the divorce he went through during the year and the fact that he wasn't going to see his wee lassie until nearly the New Year. It hadn't really been a bad break-up, Tony, and his ex-wife Liz had married young and just grown apart. Their daughter Janie was seven years old, and Tony used to get to see her at weekends, but after one weekend when Liz went away with Janie and a new man, he had some pretty choice words to say to her upon her return. This led to difficulties, and it was agreed that Tony would only get to see Janie every few weeks when Liz's mum and dad were about.

It's not as if this was going to be a permanent thing, and Tony could see the need for some boundaries, but he was still pissed off with Liz for changing the rules when it suited her. With Liz's mum and dad being away from Christmas, Liz and Janie were heading down to Liverpool to be with her man's family…so Tony wouldn't get to see Janie until the following week.

"That's terrible Tony, that's really not called for, you'd think that your ex-wife would be a bit more thoughtful than to take the wean away."

"You'd think so…but with her mum and dad heading to the sun, I can see her point."

Pauline was thinking that Tony was taking this far too mild-mannerly, and if she ever had kids, nobody would be stopping her from seeing them on Christmas Day. Things are a bit different for the mums but still, Christmas is about the weans isn't it?

"So have you got a lot of stuff lined up for next week?"

"Aye well…we'll be having a Christmas Dinner together; my mum is going to come over as well to see her."

"So what have you bought her?"

"Just some dolls and fashion accessories at the moment, see because I knew I wasn't seeing her on Christmas Day, my heart hasn't been in it. I'm going to wait until the Sales begin and then I can get more for my money…hopefully put her old man in a better light."

"I'm sure the wean loves you Tony, you don't need to be put in a better light."

"Ach, you're probably right, but you just never know do you?" At that moment, Tony moved his attention away from Pauline because he felt a tear welling up in his eye and he didn't want to be seen in that sort of state. However, just as he did, who did he see at the other side of the seated area but Liz, his ex-wife. Tony knew she was meant to be in Liverpool, the wean had told him they were due to leave the previous night, and Tony's blood was boiling.

"I'm sorry Pauline, you'll need to excuse me for a minute" said Tony as he rose quickly and marched across the seated area. Thankfully Liz saw him coming and was ready with her response; "Tony…what a surprise, look before you say anything sit down, our plans changed, the trip was cancelled."

This completely took the wind out of Tony's sails, and before he could even sit down, Liz continued; "He was a prick. A lying prick and I dumped him, so it's just me and the wean now. I know I should have said, but I didn't know what was for the best..you might have made other plans, and I didn't want to ruin them" and there was an air of genuine sympathy in Liz's voice. Even though he had no desire to be back with her, Tony was still fond of Liz, and he could tell when she was hurting. It was usually him who put her in this sort of mood, but on this occasion, his conscience was clear.

"So where is Janie?"

"She's on the ice-rink with her pal Kirsty, I took the two of them out for the day to try and make it up for not going down South. We'll probably head for a McDonalds when they're done…would you like to come…you can bring your date."

"She's not my girlfriend, she's just a work colleague, there's a bunch of us here from work."

"It's fine Tony, I'm just glad to see you out, and about with folk…I'm sorry you got messed about a bit…I truly see that now after putting up with that toerag. If you've no plans for tomorrow, you're welcome to come over to mine for your dinner, the wean will love that."

"I don't know Liz…I've not really got much stuff for her yet as I wasn't seeing her until next week, I was waiting for the sales to get her a lot more gifts."

"You were always the practical one Tony…we'll sort that out, I can put some of mine aside for you and we'll do a swap later, she knows that Santa is dropping off presents at granny's house so she'll be getting presents all next week too. It'll not be a big meal the morra, but I got some turkey, and I rattled Iceland this morning so there'll be loads of wee nibbles and stuff, it'll be fine. So what do you say?"

It was a tough decision for Tony even though it was no decision at all, getting the chance to spend Christmas with the wean changed everything…he had to say aye. "Aye Liz, I will come over, thanks…you wanting another coffee?" "I'm fine here Tony, go back to your date and when Janie is done I'll come and get you."

It was perhaps one of the problems in their marriage, but Tony always did as Liz told him, so he headed back to Pauline who was still sitting there, draining the last of her coffee. "So you're a dark horse…you moved right in there, did you pull?"

Tony was slightly bemused at the fact that everyone seemed to think he had plenty of women on the go when he had none but replied "that is my ex-wife, and it turns out the Scouse louse is a prick, so they're not down there for Christmas. I'm getting to spend the day with my wee lassie Pauline"

"That is brilliant news Tony, I'm delighted for you, are things okay between you and Liz?"

"She's got another guy to hate more than me at the moment, so I'm out of the firing line. That won't last forever, but while it does, I'll take advantage. When Janie and her wee pal finish skating we're going to grab something to eat do you want to come with us? It'll not be fancy, McDonalds or something for the weans."

Pauline immediately felt uncomfortable and was humming and hawing. She had liked Tony and had maybe thought that there could be some mileage in him but going for a meal with his ex-wife on Christmas Eve didn't seem like a fantastic starting point; "Nah, it's a family thing Tony, you go see your wee lassie and catch up" trailed off Pauline, even though she knew it was for the best.

"Don't be silly, Janie's pal is coming too and having another adult around would be good. C'mon you saved me from that gang of neds earlier, come save me from two seven year old's and a loopy ex-wife."

"Well, all girls just want to be wanted Tony so how can I refuse…but the dinner's on you…and I'll be going large with the meal."

"Ach why not Pauline, tis the season" and the pair laughed…in the space of a couple of hours Tony's plans had changed dramatically, and it was beginning to feel a lot like Christmas.

She'll Be Your Mirror

"I'm telling you Etta, I'm right at the end of my tether at the moment."

It was a sentence that Etta commonly heard from her colleagues two or three times a day, but the reasons were never the same. Sadie was often quick to complain about being at the end of her tether, so much so that Etta thought that Sadie's tether only reached as far as the end of her nose, but she continued with her story.

"It's my Kathleen Etta, she's nothing but a ned, a wee hairy, honestly, I don't know how she has turned out like this."

This was certainly a new one for Etta as she thought about the passing of time. It didn't seem that long ago since Sadie was complaining about her Kathleen not walking or talking quickly enough, about her not settling in at school or how she couldn't sit still for five minutes. There was also that time of the nits infection at the school, but Sadie insists that Kathleen never kicked that off but it wasn't a topic of conversation that was brought up too regularly. All of they troubles were overcome eventually, and Etta was convinced that this one wouldn't pose too many long-term troubles either.

"She's only 15 Sadie, its all part of growing up; here I remember you were a bit of a tearaway at that age as well were you not?"

"Me?" said Sadie, shocked at the cheek of the response but just before a follow up defence could be laid in front of Etta, a reply came in quickly shutting down any possible defence.

"I think you forget we go way back Sadie…not too many shops in the Pollok Centre survived without having their takings dip because of you and your light fingers back in the day. I even remember the time you got caught and the next day you went and nicked a bunch of flowers from Imries to give to your mum, god rest her hen she was a good woman, to apologise."

"Aye, well that's just the thing Etta, at least I knew I had done wrong and would apologise, Kathleen, nothing, no sorry mum, she just sits and sulks in her room."

That didn't sound any different from any other teenager in the world, but of course, Etta was past that stage with her two youngest growing up and very proud of them she was. Shane has been heading up a call centre team in town, and young Stacey is doing a HNC at Cardonald College, they might never run the world, but they'll hopefully pay their way, which was all that Etta was asking for from her kids. That and not to steal flowers, they were the two main aims that Etta had for her weans.

"So Sadie, what has she been doing? Running with a knife gang? Consorting with all sorts on the internet? Planning to bring down the Debenhams in Silverburn?"

"Naw, don't be stupid, just neddy things. Me and my Tony bought her some lovely clothes, best of gear, and she hasn't even worn them, its trackies and hoodies all the time. And last week, she came in with a drink in her."

Etta was unable to hold in her laughter; "a 15 year old lassie in the South Side of Glasgow has been drinking, get on the phone to the procurator fiscal. I seem to recall we were running about with hair lacquer and milk at that time with the boys taking the glue and you're worrying about your lassie having a drink. I know its illegal Sadie but have you had your brain wiped out since you were that age. On that surface of it, she doesn't sound as rough as we were....and there's a lot mair temptations for weans nooadays."

"Look Sadie, I don't want her turning out like me, like us. I mean this place, it's no what we dreamt for ourselves was it? Awright, the chances of two lassies fae the edge of Pollok marrying the guys fae Wham"

"…the chances of any lassie marrying one of the guys fae Wham" butted in Etta to give the two a right good belly laugh before Sadie continued;

"That was never going to happen, and I've done well with my Tony, you know I'm happy, but I want mair for my Kathleen than folding linen all day and only having the lunchtime chat and a couple of fag breaks to look forward to all day, that's no a life. I don't want her life to turn out like mine but at the moment, it's like looking in a mirror at times when I see her and think back on myself."

It's never pleasant to have your life so brutally laid out in less than a minute, but Etta could see where Sadie was coming from. It wasn't a miserable life, a busy working week, a few nights in front of the TV, a bearable few hours doing the housework and then you had the weekend to yourself.

That may not be the best life in the world, but it was far from the worst, and Etta wasn't too pleased about Sadie running it down….there must have been something else eating away at her, she was never one to get too defeatist about her life, she had a better social life than half the young things, her and that Tony were never out the bowling club!

"And the thing is Etta, I got a letter in, I have to attend the school with her the morra afternoon, she'll not tell me what she's done, but that can't be good can it?"

And therein lies the point of her story, with lunchtime nearly up. If that bloody Sadie could have gotten to the point the way she gets to the bottom of a Bacardi and coke this would have been wrapped up long ago but as it was, the buzzer to head back to the shop floor was about to go.

"So you going then?"

"Aye hen, I'm coming in early tomorrow morning and then finishing up a wee bit earlier, you'll be on your tea yourself the morra."

"No bother hen, I'll hear how it went the next day….chin up, it'll be nothing, maybe they've found some of the graffiti you did on the tables, and it's really you they want to see."

On the way into school, Sadie felt uneasy at what her daughter did to require her to be called in, but the nearer she approached the school, the more she felt about her own school days. It's funny how much you forget with the passage of time, but the chat with Etta the day before had brought plenty of memories flooding back. There had been some moments throughout her school days when the teachers must have been close to breaking down. PE was a terrible class for Sadie with numerous swimming pool dunkings and other pupils clothes being thrown in the showers, but that was nothing compared to the havoc Sadie and her pals would cause in chemistry.

For the one or two pupils in a school year who would hold an interest in chemistry and the fusion and interaction of atoms, chemistry was of value, but for everyone else…well, there are probably still walls in the school that bear the marks of explosions, bad reactions and the constant alchemy of turning humdrum lessons into fun times.

Miss Kennedy may not have agreed with that though, and it wouldn't have surprised Sadie if Sweaty Betty as she had been dubbed, had been carted away to the mad house. It was an unforgiving time and no place for a teacher fresh out of her probation days.

Kathleen was waiting for her mum in the main hall and for what seemed like the millionth time; she was replying "I don't know" to the only question her mum had asked her in three days. Mother and daughter walked to the headmaster's office where the school secretary let them in while waiting for Mrs Scott to come in and meet them. Sadie hadn't met the headmistress at the school yet, but if Kathleen and her pals comments were anything to go by, she was an angry old boot. Mind you, you wouldn't have got a headmistress in charge of a school back in Sadie's day, but the reminiscing was brought to a halt when the door opened, and the headmistress walked in.

"You......Sadie Shears.... I never knew...I never knew at all, this makes your daughter's success all the more surprising" was a bombshell as Sadie was transported back to her own school days and came face to face with her old nemesis. Sweaty Betty had come a long way, both women being thrown by the fact that their surnames had changed since those confrontational days long ago. In fact, the sight of the former chemistry teacher was so surprising that Sadie had managed to overlook the fact that it seemed as though Kathleen was to be praised as opposed to chastised. Mind you, the new revelation seemed to have derailed the headmistress as well.

"I never thought I'd clap eyes on you again, the amount of trouble you caused, Lainie Halston never got her eyebrows back after your experimentation, that poor girl. And as for the amount of beakers you smashed.....I'm surprised that you're still around, so I expect I must give you some credit for that."

All the while, Kathleen was fighting a losing battle to keep the smile off her face. All this time her mum had been on her case, and it turns out that Sadie was 10 times the rascal that Kathleen had ever been. The reason for the meeting was to announce that Kathleen was being sent as the school representative in a spelling competition at the Scottish Parliament the following month.

Kathleen had intended to tell the mum the reason for her attendance in school, but it was hard to get a word in edgeways between the constant criticisms. Yes, Kathleen had been hanging around with a slightly wilder crowd in recent times but it was just a way of letting off steam. Now though, it seems as though Kathleen's wild days were a walk in the park compared to her mum's antics, which removed the point and joy in rebelling against her parents.

The rest of the meeting went by in a haze with Sadie curling up with embarrassment, desperate to get out of the room and away from Sweaty Betty. It had dawned on Sadie that she had clearly been too harsh on her daughter and was all set to cut her some more slack but before she could open her mouth in the playground, Kathleen butted in;

"Look mum, I'm sorry if I've been a bit off recently, it's just been a bit of a crazy time, I'll try and pull it in a bit, sorry if I've let you down." Sadie was welling up as she looked down at her daughter, realising that she didn't have anything to worry about with respect to the path her daughter was taking, after all if Sadie could be the youngster she was and turn out a daughter like Kathleen, she'll do just fine.

The Blane Valley Death Song

It was Christmas Eve, and it seemed like the whole of Glasgow City Centre had an extra festive buzz about it. Just like that warm tingle you get from a glass of wine or a whiskey before stepping out the door on a frosty night, there was excitement and a feeling that something remarkable was about to happen. Not inside the Blane Valley pub though…it may have been Christmas Eve, but it was just like any other Saturday night. The same faces were found in the same spaces all waiting for their turn to come up at the karaoke. Sometimes the running order changed and every so often, a song would be changed or a familiar singer would be unable to attend, but the night tended to run like clockwork. There was an order about the karaoke sessions in the Blane Valley, and that was just the way that the patrons liked it. The anniversary of the birth of many people's Lord and Saviour was not going to get in the way of Jeannie from Cranhill belting out "Black Velvet".

As it was Christmas Eve though, there were some unfamiliar faces hanging around the bar area. It is the sort of night when many people may pop out for a drink after work or decide to enjoy themselves in a way that they wouldn't normally. There were one or two seats available in the pub, but it was made clear that these seats were not for people like them. Some bars and clubs can seem like a chess board where certain people are only allowed in certain sections, or they are only allowed to move in certain directions. There was also a clear seniority of the different people in the seated area but no matter what the rank the people in the seats were, they outranked those who were standing at the back. After all, if you started letting in the outsider to relax and enjoy yourself, what sort of night would you end up with?

"Do you think there's any chance of Christmas karaoke songs the night? I really fancy belting out that 'Fairytale of New

York' with my Kenny….it's really funny when we do the swearing bit" asked one of the outsiders to a barmaid but the response was notably lacking in Christmas spirit.

"Nah, there'll be none of that in here tonight..anyways is that song no a wee bit Timmy? We have to watch ourselves…this is a city centre pub open to everybody, we'll no be encouraging anything that can cause any bother" rolled out of a mouth which looked as though it had been sucking the limes that should have been gracing the gins and vodkas of the patrons.

Disappointed, Shirley turned away from the bar to be greeted by a Bernard Matthews lookalike grabbing the microphone. It would have made the night a bit more seasonal if they had hired the famous turkey killer, but sadly it turned out to be the compere of the evening and he was not shy at singing a song or two. Or five. If you felt the days of "it's my baw and I'll go home if I don't play" were behind you when you left the school playground, you were sadly mistaken. Every karaoke session hosted by Dangerous Dave saw him unleash "Shine" by Take That on the completely expecting masses. It may have been one of the songs that soundtracked the resurgence in popularity of Take That, but you get the feeling the dangerous one only learned it through those mind-numbingly awful Morrisons adverts. Dave was certainly infusing the song with the passion you would expect from a man who had got lost while looking for the chunky Kit-Kats.

"This is awful Kenny, I was wanting a Christmas night…can we not go somewhere else?" asked Shirley but the pause before she received an answer said everything. Kenny eventually got round to replying "We've not long got these drinks in love and then we were only going to have one more before we left. We can get the 62 outside…let's just make the most of it eh hen? Why not imagine the shine he is singing about is the shining of the star that hung above the stable."

Shirley refused to dignify the thought that Mark Owen may have been responsible for guiding the three wise men on their journey with an answer and returned to her rum and coke. It was nice to be out in town at this time, her and Kenny didn't usually get a chance, but it was just that Shirley was wanting a wee bit more of a festive vibe to the night. Tomorrow will be a lovely day for the weans, but it would have been great to have some grown up Christmas time…heck, it would have been nice to get a seat. Shirley nearly got a seat, but it turned out a few lassies were outside having a smoke and the seats weren't genuinely free.

The evening continued with a run of songs that seemed to get blander with every passing track:

Johnny from Drumchapel singing that Bon Jovi song about being halfway there.

Kelly and her da from the Calton singing "Nothing's Gonna Stop Us Now"

Gary from Nitshill singing "It's a Kind Of Magic" and then some wee lassie with a surprisingly okay version of "Puppet On A String".

With that Shirley got the final round of the night in and had now given up on her Christmas wishes and was hoping for a couple of upbeat numbers to allow her to dance. The rum had kicked in and even though there was no chance to heading off to a club, not at her age, having a wee shimmy wouldn't be a lousy way to kick off the Christmas period.

And with immaculate timing, Shirley's hopes were dashed when Dangerous Dave returned to this mic; "Right folks, that was a couple of good wee numbers there, so we're going to slow the pace down now." Shirley's edible gasp of "oh for fu…" was thankfully interrupted by Dave continuing with "You all know this song, it's one of the special songs in the

BV and we have a special woman for you. It's Mary, and she's going to sing Paper Roses"

Shirley's head collapsed into her hands at the cruel taunting of her hopes with a song that manages to be banal and turgid in equal measures, but as Mary prepared to sing………….

The lights went out, the power went down, and the bar was illuminated with the soft glow of candle lights. After the initial shouts and cries of "haw", "hey" and "whats going on here?" a silence filled the room which was eventually punctured by the sour faced barmaid.

"RIGHT EVERYBODY…DON'T PANIC!!! Jimmy is having a look at the fusebox, stay where you are, we cannae sell drink until the powers back on, but you can keep drinking or pop out for a fag if you want."

A general murmur and chatter started back up in the pub, but with the shimmering glow of rum giving her a bit of confidence, Shirley realised this was her chance to turn the night a bit Christmassy. Taking one last gulp for courage, she burst into song:

"You better watch out
You better not cry
You better not pout
I'm telling you why…." and as if by magic, other voices joined in with "Santa Claus is coming to town…Santa Claus is coming to town…SANTA CLAUS IS COMING TO TOWN"

A cheer went through the pub, but the mass sing-along was well underway and before Shirley could grab a breath, the whole song had been run through. There was spontaneous applause with a few cheers and claps before Dangerous Dave saw a chance to grab centre stage again…even if there was no spotlight.

"Right folks…there's still no power yet but let's keep the singsong going" before launching into a pub singer version of Rudolph the Red Nose Reindeer. It took another three Christmas songs before the lights came back, and when they did, Dangerous Dave knew that he was beaten and turned the rest of the evening over to Christmas karaoke songs.

"Right Kenny, that's us done..let's make a move." "Are you sure darling?" came the response, "You got your Christmas songs on, we can stay for one mair if you want?" Shirley put her hand in Kenny's and said, "Nah, I got what I came for, that was nice…let's get that bus and get up the road eh?"

And with that, the unfamiliar couple left the pub and left the regulars to their irregular night of Christmas fun and merriment…even if Dangerous Dave was privately seething about being robbed of his grandiose "Sweet Caroline" finale.

You're No Peeing Son

No matter your background, status, ambitions or desires in life, the need to take a pee is the great leveller. The real difference comes in how you to choose to exercise the need to urinate. As much as it is something natural and relevant to us all, urinating is definitely a practice that is better undertaken alone. Okay, if you're into that sort of thing it could be a group activity, but on the whole, you do it yourself and get back to what you were doing.

At least this is what Tommy McInnes thought. That was before he bought his home on Stanmore Road. Tommy had always been a south-side boy and with the big Asda, the motorway extension and of course, Hampden Park on his doorstep, where better for him and the wife to ease themselves into their later years.

All those years of being a football fan and going to the games had coloured Tommy's memories though. He wasn't one for going to the games much these days but he was more than happy to watch the games on television, and with Hampden just down from the house, he could savour the atmosphere as well. Well, that his opinion before he moved in, but it didn't take too long for Tommy to change his mind about football in the present day. A lot of people think that modern day football has been ruined by the players, but for Tommy, his love of the modern day game has been soured by the fans.

Who could blame him? Every big game at Hampden, fans marching by his house, tossing in their chip paper wrappers, their discarded beer cans and every now and again, peeing in his garden. This was the show stopper thought Tommy. "Animals….bloody animals" was his comments when he saw the first one taking a leak in his garden and who could blame him. Common household pets are taught to do their business in the garden and here we have grown men doing the exact same. It had gotten too much for Tommy and nowadays, he dreaded the massive games at Hampden with the Scotland games being the worst.

The present day experience of back to back international games left no time to recover or forget about the bad memories from a few days before. Tommy had grown to despise the football fans traipsing past his door, and even though he and his sons had trailed the same route on many occasions over the years, he certainly never behaved in such a fashion.

News that the international fixture list had provided Scotland with two homes games in a row, on a Saturday afternoon and Tuesday evening had Tommy contemplating getting away for a break.

"C'mon love, we'll get away for a week, avoid all the games." Sadly, Tommy's wife had other plans that weekend and then there was a hospital appointment on the Monday to think about. No, Tommy would be stuck at home for another double-header where his home would be under siege again. The rain was pouring down from the heavens, but that hadn't seemed to put a dampener on the fans that were turning up at Hampden in their droves. It was the first game of the campaign, so optimism was as high as it was ever going to get. Then again, whether hopes were high or low, whether expectations were sky high or in the gutter, the Scottish fans would be partaking in a drink. The kilt and Timberland brigade were on the booze win or lose, and it was this that caused the problems in the paths to the ground. The fans who made a quick pit-stop in town or in the more local pubs found that they had misjudged their ability to hold their water, which needed to be relieved before they got to the ground.

It wasn't that Tommy was against drinking, in his day you could take a carry out into the game with you, and there were times when peeing on the terracing was a healthier idea than risking the toilets but that was different. Peeing on someone's property was certainly a massive difference and when Tommy saw two lads loitering in front of his garden, he was up and out of his seat like Joe Jordan rising at the back post. From time to time, passers-by stopped to look at Tommy's flowers or the garden ornaments, but there was no chance that these two supporters were admiring the horticultural show Tommy had put together. One of the fans was finishing up when Tommy threw his door open, leaving his pal occupied on the other side of the hedge.

"You better no be peeing son" shouted Tommy, racing from his doorstep in an attempt to apprehend the lout but before he could get there, the fan was in full flow and there was no point in getting any closer. Tommy didn't like the idea of having his garden soaked in lager and God knows what else but he drew the line at getting covered himself. He stopped which led the fan to laugh and as he finished up, he shouted over to Tommy.

"Up yours granddad, we're supporting the national team, what are you doing?"

Tommy looked to his right, where his neighbour James was at his door watching it all unfold.

Tommy shouted over, "every time James…every time…it's a disgrace." James shook his head, shouted "shocking" and went back inside his house, perhaps fearful that his presence would see his garden become the next one to be the beneficiary of an unplanned watering.

Shocking indeed thought Tommy, and it was this that stuck in his mind for the rest of the day. Not that Scotland did anything on the park to dislodge this thought, it was another bore draw. In some ways, this was a positive result as it meant the subdued crowd sloped and slumped out of Hampden quickly, none pausing to relieve themselves on the way past. It may have been a shame the way the national team ripped the pish out of the emotions of the fans, but Tommy was finding it hard to feel empathy for the same supporters.

The next morning, Tommy was still dismayed at the thought of those fans defacing his garden and how he would love to get them back for their shocking behaviour. It was then that Tommy had hit upon the perfect idea to protect his home and have some fun with the louts.

A lifetime working with cars, sometimes professionally, others for the love of it, allowed Tommy to have an understanding of wiring and the ability to place his hands on a spare car battery with the minimum of fuss. It was a crazy idea, but the smug look on the face of that fan on Saturday had dug into Tommy's soul. Here was the home he had worked hard to afford and worked even harder to keep it looking nice in his old age. On the odd pleasant days we get, there was nothing better than Tommy and the wife sitting in the garden, and on the even odder occasions when the kids came to visit with the grandchildren, they could run about in the garden too. No, enough was enough, it was time for action.

In the garage, equipped with 40 years' experience, a box of tools, a big car battery, various components and a couple of print-outs from the internet, Tommy set to work. The work went smoothly, Tommy creating a mini wiring between two small points to ensure he was on the right lines. He tested it, tested it and re-tested it, ensuring the impact was noticeable.

Monday was a day off as he spent the day in the hospital waiting with his wife as she had numerous tests taken. There was nothing overtly wrong with Mrs McInnes, just old age and whatnot. Tommy was preparing his Tuesday night surprise for her as much as him, but a day at the hospital can be a draining affair so on their return, he spent a quiet evening in with her. Corrie, Eastenders and all the other rubbish were on but Tommy's thoughts, like most men in the country, were turning towards Tuesday and the next crucial game at Hampden.

During the day, as work was skived or pints were sunk, Tommy was working away, finishing off the adjustment he made to his fence. He decided to play slightly fair and erected a signpost just inside the garden.

"THIS IS NOT A URINAL, DO NOT STOP HERE TO PEE"

Later that evening, as Tommy finished off his tea and noted that the crowd was starting to pick up in numbers; the vast majority of fans were walking by. More than ever, fans were stopping in front of his garden, but this time, rather than behaving despicably, they were laughing. The sign itself was proving to be a deterrent, helping to keep the fans onside. Tommy was starting to wonder if he had been a bit hasty with his plans, perhaps he was missing the humour and good-natured element of the crowd, but not long before kick-off, his mood was turned again.

Hampden queues rarely move fast so when you're on Stanmore Road less than ten minutes before kick-off, you are often in trouble. Most fans were rushing by the garden, but one fan stopping so abruptly in front of the hedge grabbed Tommy's attention. By the time Tommy had got to the door, the fan was still there, and it had been obvious he was no longer just admiring the sign. In fact, he was blatantly ignoring the message of the sign, leading Tommy to shout; "I wouldn't do that son", which was quickly rebutted with, "Sorry mate, I'm bursting" and with that, the fan was thrown backwards from the fence and out into the middle of the road.

With very little traffic allowed on the streets around the game, there was no danger of the fan being endangered by a passing car, but if he was hoping to not be embarrassed, he was out of luck. He may have been flat on his back in the middle of the road, but his bladder was still doing the terribly necessary task of emptying itself, pretty much over himself to be fair.

Eventually, one of his mates came to lift him up and get him back on his feet. Kilts can hide a multitude of sins, but this was one foot soldier that was going to have some explaining to do over the course of the evening. The fan came to and was on the warpath, but his mate could be heard saying "c'mon, we'll miss the game, we'll sort it after."

Tommy stood back in amazement, partly at his own invention with a couple of wires and a car battery and partly at the state of the fan who was making his way to the stadium dripping in his own urine. Tommy sloped back inside the house until the crowd had made its way into the game and then nipped out. Ignoring the game that was underway, he dismantled the makeshift electric fence and took down the sign. The components were placed back in the garage, and the sign was shoved into the bottom of the recycling bin.

Tommy watched the rest of the game, another boring draw which had practically killed off Scotland's qualification hopes before they had seriously begun and waited. He was sure there would be a knock at the door…or worse. There was nothing though. Nothing that night, nothing the following day and as the days and weeks passed, Tommy thought about the incident less and less. The following month brought two away international games which at least brought the fans back to his mind but again, there was to be no follow-up or any more said about it.

In reality, Tommy knew he had been lucky, there could have been an interesting claim made by the fan but then again, would you be so keen to incriminate yourself? Two wrongs don't make a right, and if the fan wanted to complain about the shock treatment therapy Tommy had delivered, he would be admitting his own public urination offence. With the polis banding about chat of being put on the registrar for having a tinkle in public, anyone in their right mind would decide that letting bygones be bygones would be the preferred tactic.

Tommy went back to putting up with the fans as opposed to teaching them a lesson but any time a commentator went on about another shocking Hampden performance, he could only look back and laugh.

Made in the USA
Charleston, SC
16 November 2014